Tornado Days

Also by Christine Todd

Pins

Tornado Days

Christine Todd

RED ANEMONE BOOKS

TORNADO DAYS

Published in the United States by Red Anemone Books Inc., Chicago

ISBN: 978-0-9831888-6-5

First published in the United States: May 2013
First eBook Edition: May 2013

Some of the stories in this collection have appeared in slightly different form in the following publications: "Deadlocked" in *The Yellow Room*, 2008, "R.I.P." and "Birdcage" in the Leaf Books anthologies *Imagine Coal*, 2007, and *Discovering a Comet*, 2008.

Cover Design by Dotti Albertine

**RED ANEMONE
BOOKS**

RedAnemone.com

For Jean-Michel

CONTENTS

Things alter for the worst spontaneously,
if they be not altered for the better designedly.

–Sir Francis Bacon, 1561-1626

DEADLOCKED

Awoman sat in the dark at the back of the store. She did not move, even when she saw that he brandished a gun. He stared at her through the shadows, unnerved by her calmness, wishing he could see her clearly. He had told her to get the money out of the cash register. Nothing. He shouted out: "You'd better move, and move fast." She didn't flinch. Now what? He moved slowly toward her, still pointing the gun.

Her enormous bulk was wrapped in a gaudy sundress. Huge strawberries organized into wide stripes lay on a dazzling white background on yards of fabric. She was albino. The pinkness of her eyes was intensified by the redness of the strawberries on her dress. She scanned him without a hint of curiosity.

A sense of the ridiculous swept over him, yet he could not pull the trigger, or run, or find a way out at all. Gazing in wonderment at her ghostly skin, cream-colored hair, and gently oscillating eyes, he held the gun tighter, raising it with unsteady hands onto the glass counter that separated him from her.

"You must think you're somethin' pretty special sittin' there ignoring me when there's a gun pointed at your face," he drawled.

Rose wanted to shout, "Who do you think you are coming into my store and acting like you own me?" Instead, she donned her blank face and sat firm. Amongst her cherry pies, frosted donuts, and monster size cookies, she felt protected. No sunshine oozing in from the store's red-shuttered windows could slither beyond the long dim aisles to feign a loving, warm caress of her tender skin. No golden ray of sunlight fingering its way through the store's red front door could poke at her eyes. No nub of a man could cause her to flinch.

Goosebumps skittered down Jimmy's back. The idea that she could see right through him—that she actually knew him—crept into his head. He stifled a shudder. He'd better get himself together in a rush because he'd be damned if he was gonna get all freaked out by some silent, creepy woman. "I TOLD YOU TO GET THE MONEY."

"Do you really think I'm going to help you steal from me?"

Her sweet, high voice surprised him. It rang into his ears like a bell. He blustered, "I have a gun so I tell *you* what to do."

She leaned closer to the gun and whispered, "No you don't."

Shock raised the hair on his arms. He glanced around the shadowy store and caught sight of its barred windows. It dawned on him that on weekdays lots of people must stop in on their way to and from the expressway. Even Saturdays might get busy. Today was church day, a dead day for her business.

"How come you're open on a Sunday?"

"How come you're here on a Sunday?"

Rose's store had tempted him. With its white clapboard siding, wide porch, and quaint red shutters, it sat innocent and alone on the fringe of a small town smack dab in the middle of the Corn Belt. It should have been the perfect hit.

"You'd better move your ass and do what I tell you,

or else." A drop of sweat made its way down to his chin before plopping onto the counter. *Or else what?* An arid dryness hit his throat. He coughed loudly.

Rose pulled herself up. Ignoring his waving gun, she shuffled out from behind the counter and lumbered down the center aisle. White thong sandals flip-flopped against pale plump feet, wide hips swayed and strawberries danced before him as he followed. She was heading toward the cash register.

A smirk slid onto Jimmy's bony face. His little wiry body relaxed. After all of that drama he had won.

But Rose walked past the cash register. Fastening the CLOSED sign into the front door's high, letterboxshaped window she bent toward the lock. As the heavy deadbolt clattered into place, Jimmy realized she was locking him in. Too late, he saw her drop the key into her strawberry-covered bosom. Without so much as a glance at him, she began the trek back to the bakery counter.

Not trusting his eyes, Jimmy scuttled to check on Rose's handiwork. He tried rattling the solid wood door, and then turned in time to catch a view of her, floating like a phantom at the end of the center aisle.

He screamed: "YOU CRAZY BITCH." But she was gone. He listened for the silence to tell him that she was once more seated behind the bakery counter. Waiting for him.

Settling herself in her chair, Rose arranged the folds of her voluminous sundress before peering out into the dusky light of the store. She thought she remembered the exact moment of her birth. The dawn sky had shone a brilliant pink shot with arrows of red, a hint of white cloud laced in and around the brightest hues. When she was delivered, blood-streaked before the fiery sky, her mother rejected the sweet promise of new beginnings, but the world welcomed her, full force.

At the front of the store, Jimmy drew in deep breaths. He wished he had never set eyes on Rose, but in this battle of nerves there was no turning back. He shouted, "YOU'RE NOT GONNA GET AWAY WITH THIS."

"What am I not going to get away with?"

"WHO DO YOU THINK YOU ARE?"

"Who do you think *you* are?"

"Somebody better than you, that's for damn sure."

She remembered being seven-years-old, in their dinky town's Independence Day parade. From the end of a line of Brownies she saw her father on the sidewalk, watching. She shouted, "Dad," but he seemed unable to hear her. She shouted again and again, shame peppering her face with a heat far worse than the sun's. As she marched past he turned his back to her, prefer-ring to stare at nothing at all.

"YOU'RE NOT GONNA MESS WITH ME LIKE THIS." Jimmy was reluctantly working his way back to the bakery counter.

Sometimes, Rose imagined that she was born with flaming red hair, bright cheeks, and deep, dark eyes. There was something about her life that had drained her of color.

"YOU are not going to ignore ME," Jimmy whined.

Rose sighed. Back on her feet, she walked toward the center aisle and rounded the corner.

Jimmy puffed himself up like a bantam rooster. This woman was not gonna get the better of him. He'd force her to hand over the goddamn door key even if he had to tear off her stupid clothes to get it. His skin prickled at the thought.

Rose faced him squarely, feet planted. "I am never going to help you do this to me."

Jimmy's heart hammered so hard he thought she could hear it. He pulled himself up to his full height. "Get the fuckin' key and open the cash register."

Her eyes barely oscillated.

"Get me that money NOW." He wanted to smack her, hard.

"People have much that you can steal from them, the least of which is money."

Jimmy hesitated. *What the hell is she talking about?* A smarmy smile surfaced. "Well then, get me your money if it's no big deal."

Rose began to rearrange shelves, placing bottles of hot pepper sauce next to cans of baked beans, straightening rows of tomato ketchup bottles alongside jars of chunky salsa.

Jimmy snorted. "I soon shut you up, didn't I?"

Red wine vinegar slid into perfect lines, Rose's clean white hands working quickly and efficiently. "I prefer a tidy life," she said. "I like order, neatness, all of the ends tied."

Jimmy blinked hard, his eyes glittering.

"I make my own choices," she added, turning to face him.

"Oh yeah? Well, *my* choice is for *you* to get me the money."

"That's not your choice to make. Besides, I've already made up my mind."

"We'll see about that."

"Are you happy?" she asked, gazing into his face.

Jimmy's brains clashed about trying to anchor down reality. This Looney Tune was trying to *chitchat* like he was her *girlfriend* or something.

"What's it to you?" he retorted.

She shrugged. "I thought that if you were happy, you wouldn't be doing this."

"I'LL BE HAPPY WHEN YOU GET ME THE MONEY."

"Then you're never going to be happy."

"That cash is worth everything to you, ain't it?"

"I think you know it's not about the money."

"IT'S ALWAYS ABOUT THE MONEY."

"You have a lot to learn."

Ice grew in his bones, freezing his skin from the inside out. Chilling thoughts broke through. Was he standing here talking to a ghost? Was she afraid of nothing because she was dead already? His heart thumped louder.

"Jesus Christ lady, just open the goddamn register."

She stood akimbo. "Open it yourself."

Before boxing her life down to the floor space con-tained in her store, Rose occasionally ventured out for walks. She remembered coming across a primrose that had pushed its way through the main road's surface to show itself off to no one in particular. Velvety scarlet petals and bright green leaves stretched up and out of black tarmac to experience as much of the world as possible for as long as possible. It hadn't worried about murderous vehicle wheels. No fear was great enough to keep it buried. That flower had determined to live its life fully, bravely, if only for itself. Rose marveled at its courage.

White-faced, Jimmy corralled his bravado. "I'M NOT GONNA LOSE THIS GAME," he bellowed.

"We can stop anytime you choose."

"Don't make me shoot you."

"Nobody is making you do that."

"You're pushing for it."

"No. You are."

He thought he saw a glint of triumph in her eyes, and believed a smirk had raised her mouth. Had she guessed that he'd never shot anyone before? His insides sizzled and burned. He snarled, "If you don't get the money and open that door, I'll shoot for that fuckin' key myself." He aimed the gun at her chest. "This should be about right."

Rose adjusted her stance, turning slightly to her right and standing tall. "It just might be."

She smiled so sweetly, Jimmy's insides hurt. He opened his mouth so speak. But what could he say? He knew she was never gonna do what she was told. Not ever. And he couldn't slink out, especially now.

Furious that she had him cornered he pulled the trigger like a madman, sending her the promised hail of bullets in a deafening spray.

He watched as she staggered two steps back before falling to the floor with a great clatter. His heart skipped and jumped and he labored to breathe. He wondered if anyone had seen him come into the store, any person who could finger him, get him locked up.

He hoped nobody heard the shots; prayed that he wouldn't hear a hammering on the door and a voice shouting, "Everything all right in there?" A rivulet of urine stained the right leg of his jeans as it made its way toward his shoe. Sweat streamed from every pore. "Jezuzz Christ Almighty," he cried. "Why did you make me do this?"

A huge release of blood began to flood the center aisle. Rose lay on her back with arms outstretched as though to embrace him. But it was her eyes that he would never forget. No longer oscillating, steadily fixed on his even as she fell, her eyes burned into his. Jimmy stared back, wondering what she was saying to him.

He hadn't noticed her dress. It lay in soft folds, spread out like wings against the pale floorboards. Acting as a wick, it was drinking up the lake of blood surrounding her. Strawberries disappeared as the brilliant white background turned crimson.

Jimmy turned to run—getting as far as the door before remembering that Rose held the key to his escape in her bosom. A thrill of fright snaked through him, raising the hair at the nape of his neck. He turned back to the center aisle. Through the dusky light, Rose looked like an enormous red-winged angel.

Jimmy scuttled through the store seeking out an exit. He zeroed in on the wide panel of cream cotton that hung from ceiling to floor behind Rose's chair like a stage curtain. Expecting to find the back door hidden behind it, he grasped one edge of the fabric, adorning it with his grimy fingered signature. He yanked it aside, and faced a blank wall. He hugged his chest and slowly raised his head, a sense of being watched slithering over him. From a large portrait hanging high, a woman's knowing eyes looked down to challenge his. Bright flames of hair curled around rosy cheeks. A solemn red mouth attested to the idea that she was taking stock of him.

I know you, he thought, before feeling a rush of hate.

A door stood to the right of Rose's chair. He eased it open. A dimly lit staircase climbed upward, a multitude of artworks brightening its walls. He envisioned a second floor fire escape and took the stairs two at a time, coming face-to-face with himself through Rose's mirror at the top. His breath whooshed out of his lungs. He spun on his heels and flew along the hall, landing breathless in the doorway of a spacious, tidy art studio.

Above the fireplace hung a large black-framed

painting of a dark haired man with drooping shoulders, and a round blond woman in dull clothes. Side-by-side they viewed a bleak, colorless landscape, their backs to the painter. Behind them, one small scarlet flower grew in barren ground.

A shiver caught hold of Jimmy's spine. *Weird! Weird! Weird!*

In the center of the room, an enormous blank canvas leaned up against an easel like a grave before a tombstone. Along an old table, tubes of paint and brushes in jars lined up like an army of soldiers. Around the baseboards unframed works rested one against the other.

Through the nearest door, a neat, queen-size bed with its highly patterned comforter provided riotous color. It hurt his eyes so much he had to turn away.

He ran from room to room finding locked shutters and barred windows, but never a door leading outside. Sensing that something unspeakable was creeping up on him, his stomach soured. He raked shaky fingers through his stringy black hair, and told himself he'd better stay cool or he'd never get out of this hellhole.

Nerves scorched, he returned to the center aisle praying, *Please, let the key be somewhere in sight.*

It wasn't.

He stared at the hole he had blown through Rose,

and knelt beside her to begin his search. Gingerly lifting what remained of her sodden sundress's neckline, he muttered a grim, "Just do it." The pungent smell of warm blood filled his nostrils and he retched. As his hand searched Rose's tattered bra, he pictured getting out of the store and disappearing into the night on the next train. He'd find an empty boxcar to call home and ride it out of Illinois all the way to California.

Rose's blood began attaching itself to him. His white t-shirt, with its large splotches of red resembled Rose's strawberry patterned sundress. Hands trembling, he searched beneath her breasts and under the folds of her waist. Sweat dripped from his face onto hers. Horror crawled through him like a rat as he plunged both hands into her chest. Blood crept over his hands and up his arms.

He screamed: "HELP ME!" And felt the key deep inside Rose's shattered heart, lodged there when her chest was blown to pieces.

All Jimmy saw now was the way out. His black duffel bag lay in the checkout lane. When he bent to retrieve it, his eyes could not resist glancing toward the cash register and his mind could not help imagining the money it contained. He scurried behind the checkout counter, and saw the partly open cash drawer. Rose's cash register had never been locked.

That stupid freak! He yanked the drawer wide open.

Next to the small change, stacks of twenties, fifties, and one hundred dollar bills lay neatly side-by-side. Jimmy could not believe his good fortune. He tossed his bag onto the checkout counter and unzipped the side pocket. He grabbed at Rose's cash, failing to notice that his hands left red medallions on the money.

A faint air horn blast from a distant freight train filtered through the silence. He'd better catch this ride. He flung his bag over his shoulder and juggled an arm-load of bills as he made for the door.

Now he could get away safely. What happened to her didn't matter. Never did matter. Who cares if a fat smart-ass woman is dead? She asked for it, didn't she? Anyway, he'd probably done her a favor. She was alone. She was a misfit. Where were her family and friends? She probably had none. Who cares?

He shoved down the idea that he did.

In glossy hands the key slipped and slid and the stiff old deadbolt held fast. A louder horn blast set his nerves to shaking. *Jesus!* He might miss this train. He dropped his bag, jiggled the key out of the lock, and held it up for inspection.

If she'd just done what she was told her ass would still be planted in her safe little world. He'd just wanted to steal a little from her so that he could keep himself going. That's all he'd wanted. That's all.

But, what the hell had she wanted?

He ran his thumb along the edge of the key, and felt a chip, a dent, something that wasn't right.

She'd had guts though—more than he'd ever owned. She'd stood her ground, wouldn't let him bring her down. He bet that she could look at her face in the mirror most days, which was more than he could do.

He glanced around hoping to find better light, and then held the key so close to his eyes it looked blurry.

This time the horn blast was so loud he thought the train was getting close enough to roll over him. He jammed the key back into the lock. Nothing.

Pressure built behind his eyes. The key was shot. Damaged from one of those fucking bullets. One of them had nicked it just right. Exactly fucking right.

Jimmy wished he were safely settled on the floor of his California bound boxcar, his stolen cash spread out in front of him like a deck of cards, just like always.

He pictured the forlorn couple in the middle of a wasteland not noticing the flower that had somehow managed to grow. Stupid damn painting. Nothing can grow like that when the odds are stacked against it. But he knew that wasn't true. A sob caught his throat. He didn't want this stuff in his head.

Wait. Hadn't he seen a phone behind the counter?

He sprinted back to the bakery and snatched it up, his forefinger positioning itself above the dial as he dropped into Rose's chair. His eyes squeezed shut while he searched for ideas. Who could he call? He was a drifter. A loner. No friends. No family. For damn sure he couldn't call the sheriff or the fire department to get him out. They'd lock him up and throw away the key.

His breath came in great ragged gasps. He was entombed inside an old fortress and could conceive of nothing worse.

What would happen tomorrow? Would there be heavy traffic on the road outside? People stopping in for their coffees and fucking donuts and finding the place locked ... every day, each way, for a week, two weeks, more? Oh God. Then would the sheriff come calling?

He stood over Rose, her arms stretched wide in welcome, her eyes daring him.

What the hell was he supposed to do with her? Was there a cellar in this nut house? Like he could drag something this size anywhere at all let alone along this damn floor, and for how long, and then down a set of basement steps. With his luck there was no cellar anyway. He might have to beat through the floor to get to a crawl space, and there was nothing in this stupid store to help him do that.

The empty gun weighed heavy in his hand. He could swear that his last bullet was heating up in his jeans' pocket.

He heard the California train roll by, blowing its horn like mad as it crossed the main road, the noise soon fading with the distance.

He thought that if he dared look in the direction of the bakery counter, he'd see high on the wall behind it a beautiful woman with flaming hair, a solemn red mouth, and deep, dark eyes that had seen right through him. And he knew that she had won.

THE WEDDING PLANNER

Amanda saw the dress in the window of Bonnie's Bridal Boutique, a sight so luscious her mouth watered. She was on her way to an important business meeting, heels click-clacking along the sidewalk, thoughts of signed contracts for big orders playing in her brain. But the dress had shone so bright she was forced to stop and gaze awhile, mesmerized by its splendor. To hell with work, she thought, as she stepped into the store. When you see a wedding dress like this one, you just have to buy it.

Bonnie Daley, famous around town for her bridal outfitter television commercials, beamed at her from behind a delicate white lacquered desk. "Are you the bride?" she asked, rising to her feet.

A thrill ran up Amanda's spine and her scalp tingled. The Bride!

Bonnie walked toward her, right arm outstretched, her motherly face suffused with pleasure. "You don't have an appointment, so I expect it's the dress in the window that brought you in here. It's perfect for you."

In the dressing room, Amanda stood stripped down to her underwear before remembering her client meeting. It was two o'clock. Her business partner, Jake, and the rest of the team would be sitting at the conference table with their new client, each with a copy of her bound presentation lying before them. They would have started to worry.

Into her cell phone flew a text message—a barefaced lie. "Family emergency," Amanda wrote, "Please start without me."

Jake would take over the meeting. "Amanda sends her apologies, but she has a family emergency and can't make it." They would share shocked looks. There would be a murmur of sympathy. "I hope everything is all right," they would tell each other, their curiosity secretly bubbling.

"Here we are," trilled Bonnie, edging through the dressing room door with the shimmering gown held high. The dress rustled softly as she carried it in, whispering warnings that Amanda sought to catch. Her brain quickly transported her to the top of the aisle in St. Christopher's Church. She watched herself clutching her father's arm and feeling him tremble as they made their way forward. In the pews, family and friends were dabbing their eyes and whispering to one another that she, Amanda, was the perfect bride. "That man is lucky to have her," she heard them say. "Look at her dress. She couldn't have planned a finer wedding."

"First, raise your arms," instructed Bonnie, awash in good cheer. "You know, even in down times, a beautiful bride is good for the wedding business. Like they say, put a pretty woman into the perfect dress and everyone will want to know where she bought it."

The elegant sheath slid over Amanda's arms and enveloped her body in a silken cocoon.

"Oh my," said Bonnie, her eyes misty. "It's as if this gown was made just for you."

Amanda was shocked by the weight of the dress. It felt so heavy she wondered how the seams could hold it together, and pictured it falling apart at the altar. She said, "I never knew the heaviness of satin."

One of Bonnie's well-plucked eyebrows rose in

surprise. "You think this dress is heavy?" She bent to fuss with the hem. "It's light as a feather compared to most."

In front of the three-way mirror, Amanda gave an impromptu twirl. But oh, it was so very beautiful.

When she and Jake were lovers they would lie on her rumpled bed staring out at starry skies. They had talked of a future together—two kids, a house with a wide front porch, and a major dining room so they could invite their families over for Thanksgiving dinner. They were planning their wedding. She had known then that a dress like this would be worn for him.

"Wait." Bonnie produced a veil, long and flowing, delicate as gossamer, and pure white like the dress. "Let's try this," she said, arranging it carefully on Amanda's head. "I think it might be perfect."

Amanda stared at herself in the mirror. A mix of awe and joy and fear took hold, and she thought with horror that she might cry.

"What is it, Honey?" Bonnie placed a plump arm around her shoulders.

Amanda wondered if it looked like she had no mother, no sister, no one close enough to share this moment with her.

"You can talk to me," Bonnie said, "I've heard just about everything."

Amanda pulled herself together. "I just never ex-pected to find the perfect dress today."

Amanda lugged her wedding dress and veil out of her car, across the front porch, and through the front door without running into any of her neighbors, which was a good sign. Such items were to be kept hidden from view until the day itself. Otherwise, in this small town rumors would fly. "There's been no announce-ment," people would sniff. "Who is she supposed to be marrying this time?"

She envisioned a cluster of married women, the local busybodies, covering their mouths like whispering schoolchildren. "Even the pretty ones have a sell-by date."

At the top of the stairs, she leaned against the banister. Her body shook from the effort of holding her dress and veil aloft to keep them from meeting the floor. They weighed more than she did. She felt sure of it.

Her four bridesmaids, childhood friends, were all married years ago and scattered around the country like tossed confetti. They want her to join their ranks.

"Last but not least," she whispered.

She opened the door to her bedroom closet, so many thoughts rattling in her ears she had to turn on the TV to help block them out. A glamorous news anchor was running through a lengthy list of tragedies, her voice a tad too bright, a tiny smile tweaking her mouth. There are terrible things happening in the world, Amanda thought, struggling to put her things away. People who report devastating news ought not to smile while doing so.

Jake had smiled from the head of the conference table six weeks ago. "Amanda and I have an announcement," he declared. "We've canceled our engagement. It was a joint decision. Enough said." The silence that followed still hurt her ears.

The dress hung like a glittering specter at the back of her closet. It was the catalyst she needed to propel her into completing her wedding plans. There would be no more dilly-dallying.

The sky was dark and spangled with stars. A chill wind crisped the air. Amanda started her car and fiddled with the heat vents, her breath puffing out like clouds. She smoothed down her black wool coat, making sure each button was fastened, before backing out of her driveway. She would be there in no time at all. If her luck held, nobody she knew would see her and ruin things.

Before today she used to visualize marrying a new

man. She used to imagine how she would feel gathering up Jake and the staff in the conference room and making her big announcement. "I'm getting married," she would say with a smile. "And, you're all invited."

Jake would try to hide his shock, his face failing to capture the necessary pleased look. (Had he thought he owned her? Had he believed she would mourn him forever?) "What a wonderful surprise," he would say, his voice trembling. "Who is the lucky guy?"

He had not phoned after work to ask about her made-up family emergency. He probably thought it best to wait until tomorrow, when they were face-to-face in the office, to judge if it was true.

Amanda pressed down harder on the accelerator. She sped up the ramp and onto the expressway, and laughed out loud to allay her fears.

Everything would be different now. This afternoon she had found her perfect wedding dress. It was a sign.

In front of Jake's apartment building she turned off the engine and stared up at the ninth floor. His lights were on. She started to unbutton her coat, slowly revealing the dress, which glimmered ghostly under the full moon.

The cold nearly stole her breath away as she hurried across the parking lot. A prick of uncertainty had to be quashed.

The dress rustled against her legs as she sped through the empty lobby. Alone on the elevator, she waited calmly as it flew up to the ninth floor without stopping. She had arrived undetected—another good sign.

In front of Jake's door she hesitated, before placing a finger over the peephole and pressing the doorbell. She was the last person he would expect to see here. Just the idea of it melted her bones.

But it was a woman who opened the door, a tall, dark-haired, attractive woman. She and Amanda mirrored the same shocked look—wide eyes, dropped jaws.

They spoke in unison, "Who are you?"

The dark haired woman laughed.

For the first time in her life, Amanda felt like a complete lunatic.

"It's not often I open the door to a bride," the woman said.

"It's not often I walk around town in a wedding dress," Amanda countered, embarrassment giving her a good wash down. "In fact, it's the first time I've ever really worn a wedding dress."

"Why are you here?"

"Does Jake still live here?"

"No. I moved in right after he left, a couple of weeks ago."

Amanda wondered if this was true. Surely he would have told her? "Do you know Jake's new address?"

The woman looked at her closely. "Do you *really* want it?" she asked.

Amanda felt shocked by the question. It had never occurred to her to ask it of herself. *Did* she really want to know Jake's address? "I'm not sure anymore," she said, feeling dazed.

She looked down at her dress, grown heavier by the minute, and wondered how she could get out of here without running into people and proving herself the town clown.

A horrible thought had settled on her. Had she been acting so crazy lately that Jake—her lost lover and longtime business partner—had secretly moved house to try and get away from her, before she could do something like *this?*

A wave of humiliation laid pressure behind her eyes. Jake had fallen out of love with her and she had acted like it was the end of her world.

The woman stuck out her hand. "I'm Kelly." She opened the door wider. "Come on in."

The apartment looked nothing like it did when Jake

lived here. It seemed bigger, brighter, and much more colorful. Not a trace of him remained.

"I changed just about everything," Kelly said, as if reading her thoughts. "I brightened everything up with paint."

Amanda had a sudden urge to paint every inch of her dull house and start brightening up her life.

"White wine okay?"

"Thanks." She managed a smile. "Maybe it will give me the courage I need to walk back out of the building in this damned dress."

Kelly poured two full glasses of Pinot Grigio and handed one to Amanda. They each took a sip.

"About that dress ..." Kelly's voice trailed off.

Amanda's cheeks flamed. "Yes?"

"I don't suppose it's for sale?"

Surprise shot through her. She stared at Kelly, who looked perfectly serious. Suspicion rose. What if this woman was really Jake's new lover, who was hoping to wear this dress at their wedding? "It might be," she said, with caution. "Why do you ask?"

"I moved here for my job. Hardly had time to think about it, really. My fiancé is moving here too. We've decided to get married this summer."

Amanda pondered this for a while. She didn't want

to do anything else on impulse, anything else she would regret.

"Your dress is exactly what I want, Amanda. It's gorgeous. And when you see a dress like this one, you just have to—"

"Well, it's brand new, you know. I've only worn it for the last half hour or so. I'd expect to get a good price for it."

"So, you'll sell it to me?"

"Do you want the veil as well?"

"Yes."

Amanda thought Jake was probably asleep right now, maybe with a new lover. Tomorrow he would come into work and feel puzzled by the change in her. It would take him a while to understand that it was finally over for her too.

Amanda felt the dress lighten. She clinked her glass against Kelly's.

"Okay then," she said.

R.I.P.

S oon, the town's newest parking lot will be striped with parallel lines in red paint: a fitting color, Maude thinks. But today its cement is wet. Wearing black rubber boots, she steps into it and starts stamping out the imprint of her first letter.

Lungs afire, she plods up and down, back and forth, making sure each footfall lands with a squish precisely where it ought to. Her fifteen minutes of fame must be worth the effort. A group of gaping children gathers, astonished to see an old woman vandalizing public property. She lifts her eyes to judge them and wonders if she'll finish her message before the police arrive, but does not speed up, planting one careful foot in front of the other until the end is reached.

Clumps of cement adorn her boots as she stands on the sidewalk admiring her footwork. Mesmerized children congregate behind her. She pictures her old house folded up like a concertina beneath the epitaph she trampled over it. Laying to rest her terrible secrets, Maude limps away, smiling.

TORNADO DAYS

He wipes his forehead and groans. The Michigan summer, hot and humid, is stifling his lungs into near submission. One of these days he'll move his ass to comfortable Arizona where the air is hotter, but so much drier he won't even know it. At least, so they say. Barney lies in the shade alongside the trailer, paws twitching and pink tongue lolling as he pants out the heat. Jack stands up on spindly legs to get him more water, and peers along the narrow dirt road and up the hillside to see if a dust cloud heralds Doc Harry's arrival. He could use a little company today, even Harry's.

"Nowhere in sight," he mutters to his wife, Barney's dry dish in hand.

Lorraine stands barefoot by the sink in a dress made from flimsy white cotton printed with deep green vines and clusters of purple grapes. Every fan they own whirs at top speed blowing steamy air her way. Her dress billows and her sun bleached hair flies. She's washing lettuce and listening to some jock on the radio spouting off about crooked politicians.

Behind her back Jack twirls his forefinger in the air and mouths, "Whoop-dee-damn-doo."

His wife picks up a cutting knife.

"It's weird out there," he says. "Tornado weather. Not even the flies can be bothered to buzz."

She chops a tomato dead center. "It's hot all right."

Jack nudges her aside with his elbow and shoves the dog's bowl under the cold water.

On the countertop Lorraine's homegrown straw-berries, cucumbers, and green onions shine in colan-ders, brightening up their kitchen with fragrance and color—a mockery that leaves him breathless. He makes his way back outside with Barney's overfilled bowl, water spilling over his hands and falling to the floor like teardrops.

He can't remember what they talked about before Zack died, before she turned quiet, saving her thoughts like a set of state secrets They used to gab for hours on end. They used to make love for hours on end. (He immediately squelches this thought.) Now, she practically lives in that garden of hers—has just about taken root there—sometimes sitting motionless under a shade tree, hour after hour, watching things grow.

Jack quickens his step as deeper memories stir. Up pops the daily vision of Lorraine, leaning over their baby's crib, wild screams pouring out of her enough to curdle milk. Even now he feels them deafening his ears, blinding his eyes, clogging his pores.

The air lies heavy with humidity. Jack feels his knees buckle under its weight. He wonders what it's *really* like in dry Arizona, and pictures those enormous cactus plants, the ones with long, sharp spikes that people can see and easily avoid.

Barney attacks the water before his bowl hits the patio's cement, sending cool waves crashing onto Jack's old sandals. Feet anointed, Jack straightens up and glares at the sky.

He had yelled: *"What have you done?"* into Lorraine's tortured face. Well, she *must* have done something stupid. Why else would Zack have stared up at her with those awful accusing eyes?

"He's here." Lorraine leans in the doorway, watching him from behind again. He hates that. It makes him
feel all shook up, as if his underbelly's showing and she
knows that it lacks proper armor. He's sure she does it
on purpose.

Together they watch the orange-brown dust cloud
that hangs on the hillside expanding in length behind
Harry's blue pickup truck.

Jack waited for Harry that day too, pacing outside
on the patio, scanning the blurred horizon beneath the
same pale, mustard-green sky, listening to his crazed
wife's sobs, knowing she held Zack to her breast trying
to feed life back into him.

That was the only time he'd wished for closer neighbors, a wise woman or two who would rush over and
spare him from witnessing anymore of the horror
inside.

When they moved to the countryside three years
ago, settling into this idyllic five-acre dip in rolling land,
their own miniature valley, they bought a brand new
double-width trailer so that Lorraine could set up her
office at home. "We'll plant a garden, and dig a well,
and get a dog, and start a family, not necessarily in that
order." They hugged a lot back then. She smelled of
shampoo and soap, a cleanness that still makes his heart
swell and his eyes sting.

"Living in a trailer, we'd better hope no tornadoes come calling."

"We'll be safe down here, they'll bounce right over us."

He hadn't known then that tornadoes come in many forms, snatching away peoples' lives, spinning them out of control forever. He and Lorraine were happily thrashing under the covers that morning. "Our cute, lazy baby is having himself a lie in," he said. Lorraine's eyes sparkled. "We have time for a quickie." It was nine o'clock before they thought to check on him.

The pain in his throat is back, burning like to damn well kill him. He'll have to ask the doc about this. Maybe today. He swallows hard, knowing that he won't.

Lorraine gives a solemn wave as Harry pulls up in front of the trailer in air-conditioned comfort, his large sad eyes seeking hers through his truck's closed windows. Jack arranges his face into what he hopes is a benign look. It's the first anniversary of Zack's last day on Earth. He bets Harry wants to score points with her by coming on all mushy.

According to Perfect Harry it was nobody's fault. Nobody's fault! The good doctor would have to say that, him being soft on Lorraine and all. Just the thought of him makes Jack's insides twist.

The truck door opens and Harry steps out carrying a baby size bouquet of tea roses, yellow and white. Perfect. He's gazing at Lorraine, who is herself gazing at the flowers, her blue eyes swimming.

Trust Handsome Harry to press the right buttons.

Jack wonders if the two of them ever get it on while he is out working his ass off at the newspaper. They could have done it in the trailer or in Harry's innocent country doctor's office, on the examination table, Lorraine's legs fastened up in those stirrup things.

Lorraine sets a tray of iced beers in the middle of the table and sits down. Harry plunks himself down to her right. Jack has no choice but to sit on her left.

Lorraine quips, "A rose between two thorns."

Harry laughs.

Jack can hardly remember the last time he saw his wife smile, yet here she lifts one out for an airing, today of all days. "There's a tornado watch all afternoon," he says, wanting Harry to leave.

Harry stares at him, "Are you all right?" A stripe of sweat shines above his pale upper lip.

"I'm fine." Jack pictures President Nixon, a man who always managed to look like the crook he claimed not to be, his lip perpetually decorated in sweat.

"You've lost a lot of weight. Too much really." Harry says this gently. He's leaning forward, looking like he might actually try and grasp his hand. "You really need to eat more."

Jack's nerves set to jangling so bad he thinks they can both see him shake. "I'm okay." He catches Lorraine flashing Harry a furtive look; her eyebrows pulled together, her head doing a miniature shake. She's contradicting him.

Harry doesn't miss a beat. "Have you two thought about moving closer to the village," he says, "It must get a bit lonely out here."

"No," Jack snaps. "This is our home."

"Is it?" he hears Lorraine murmur into her beer.

Jack wishes he could let rip with a scream, a blood curdling holler that would echo for miles around, bringing smug, satisfied people to their doors where they'd stand and scratch their heads and ask each other, "Did you ever hear anything like *that* before?"

The air hangs still and silent, shimmering with heat. The dog starts whining. Jack checks the sky and wipes his forehead with the sleeve of his shirt. "Looks dangerous up there."

Harry downs his beer. "Let's go. My basement is safer than your trailer."

"No thanks," Jack answers. "We're safe enough here." But he knows that isn't true. Nobody is safe anywhere.

"You never know with twisters," Harry persists, as if he's the be all and end all of the weather knowledge factor. "Twisters go downhill when they're in the mood."

"Not in these hills," Jack huffs.

He sees another look pass between the two of them. This is the one that says, "Jack is going downhill himself these days."

Well, guess what, Jack knows that he is, and he doesn't give a flying crap.

A wind gusts out from nowhere, cold on his skin, a chilly warning that they'd better start hunkering down. A distant siren wails.

"They've spotted one," Harry says, "It really is time to get out of here."

Jack scorns, "You'd better get rolling if you're that scared."

"At least *he's* not too scared to *live*." Lorraine stands beside Harry, her Zack eyes flashing hate at him.

"Lorraine—"

"My husband is afraid of his own shadow. Isn't that right Jack?"

"Let's go to my basement and take this up there," says Harry, grasping hold of Lorraine's elbow.

"Where's Barney?" she shouts, tears rolling.

Jack wants to tear her away from Harry and pull her close, to smell her skin and hair, to feel her breath on his cheek. His arm reaches out.

"You're such a coward." She speaks so quietly he almost misses it.

Barney cowers under the trailer, hiding from the coming storm. Harry, dog treat in hand, lies on the cement persuading him to come out.

"Handsome Harry," Jack says, "Your knight in shining armor."

"He talks to me. You don't, and when you do you are so delusional about what I'm thinking or doing."

"Every goddamn day you look at me with those eyes of yours."

"You won't talk to me!" she cries.

The wind whips up cold and foreboding, sending Lorraine's hair into a frenzy. Lightening forks on the horizon.

Harry is dragging Barney into the truck. "Come on you two," he yells.

"We'll follow behind," shouts Lorraine, cruising for a fight.

"Jack," Harry warns, "you can't stay here."

"Just go!"

They watch the truck take off, Barney panting and

yelping at them from the back seat. Harry meets Jack's eyes, registering fury, before flooring the gas pedal and streaking away.

A noise catches them, a low rolling rumble that makes Jack's skin prickle.

"Oh God," Lorraine says, "I hope Harry makes it home okay."

Jack bristles. "I hope *Barney* makes it home okay."

Her back stiffens. She opens her mouth, and then snaps it shut. He catches sight of the fire in her eyes, hellish flames that consume from within. He swallows hard. The burn in his throat is back.

They turn to the eastern horizon, the wind pelting them with dust and dirt. There, looming over the hilltop, a slender funnel spirals in the sky.

Jack gasps. "It won't dip down here, Lorraine. We're safe down here."

"No we're not."

He shrinks from the idea that they have no under-ground shelter to protect them, like the one he had promised to put in behind their trailer, beyond the shade trees, before Zack. He shields his eyes and looks every which way across their valley, hoping to find a forgotten trench or natural depression that will save them. There's nothing.

Lorraine stands watching him. Her hands, small and

strong, work to batten down her hair. It dawns on him that she's waiting for something. What?

"We can't just stand here, Lorraine."

"It's too dangerous. Right?"

His jaw tightens. "Why are we doing this?"

"Why don't *you* tell me why we're doing this?" she shouts. "Talk to me, Jack. *Talk to me!*"

He can't stop himself. "You'd rather sit in that damned garden than be with me."

"That 'damned garden' has saved me, Jack. It responds to me. It grows beautiful things out of the *dirt*."

"You pushed me away."

"What do you think you and your silence did to me?"

"Your garden is silent," he huffs.

She points downward. "I'd be buried under the dirt without my flowers and vegetables."

"You sound crazy Lorraine. You know that?"

"I don't care. It's true."

"I watch you from the kitchen window, for hours at a time."

"I know."

He grabs her arm, furious. "So, why didn't you turn to me, Lorraine? Why didn't you ask me to sit with you?"

"You need to think, Jack. *Think!*"

The wind is howling, tearing at his clothes, and nettling his legs with sharp sprays of dirt. He feels faint, and wonders if he is about to collapse in a heap at his wife's feet.

"What do you want me to say, Lorraine? Just tell me what you want."

"My god, Jack. What do you think I want?"

He yells over the wind's roar. "All right then. Go to Perfect Harry's."

"You can't outrun tornadoes," she yells back.

He starts pulling her toward her car. "You can out-run this one."

She yanks her arm away, tears flying. "I can't leave you here. All alone."

Her concern shocks him. He feels his face grow hotter than hot, and hopes she won't notice. He cranes his neck and makes a production of checking out the tornado, which is still at a distance and high in the sky. He wonders what it would be like to have it swoop down and whisk him away. Would the newspaper put his name in a headline? After all, he works there. Or would they just say something like: "Man Swept up by Tornado. Feared Lost"?

Maybe he is already lost.

Last spring he watched Lorraine plant her first

garden, all by herself. He watched her from the kitch-en's open window, birdsong filtering into the room, the stench of cow manure spiking the air. Week after week he stared out at her. She was a lone sentry, watching her garden grow: sometimes huddled beneath her umbrella weathering a rainstorm, sometimes wrapped up in blankets to thwart the cold, sometimes sitting barelegged in the sunshine. Every day she watched and waited for the birth of her beautiful harvest. He understands now that it helped her live in a world with no Zack in it.

He cannot face her. She has those eyes—blue as the sky, round like dinner plates—eyes that always manage to seek out the good stuff that she holds close to her heart.

"Did you hear what I said?" she shouts over the din.

"I can't run away, Lorraine. Not today."

The force of the wind has him wrestling with her car door. He sees his wife's right hand reaching out to help him, and is seized by a sudden crush of shame. He catches her staring at him.

Jack's mouth takes off on its own, words shooting past his gullet like bullets out of a gun. "I didn't mean it, Lorraine. I didn't mean what I said about Zack."

Lorraine lets go of the car door. Her hands cover her mouth.

"I wanted everything to be your fault, Lorraine. Then it couldn't be mine." He's crying just like her now, just like a girl. "It has to be somebody's fault, doesn't it? Otherwise, what was the *reason?*"

"We loved Zack. We did nothing wrong." She is wearing that tortured face, the one that shows up whenever she is unguarded, the one she wore while sitting alone in her garden, waiting for the harvest.

"I'm sorry, Lorraine."

She pulls him to her. They stand for a long time, arms tight around each other, feet planted against the storm. She says, "We'll always be Zack's parents. Nothing can ever change that."

She is fiercer and stronger than he remembers. His heart feels like it's going to burst over the truth in her words. His throat has eased. He feels a glimmer of hope, and lets out a sigh.

The tornado is roping out into wider curling shapes, stretching itself thinner and weaker across the eastern sky as it fades into the distance.

"Looks like that's gone for good," Lorraine says, wiping her eyes.

The heat reappears with barely a breeze to catch. Jack and Lorraine stand side-by-side surveying the damage. Their patio chairs lie off where the wind blew them, and their table is overturned against the trailer.

"We could have fixed us," Lorraine touches his arm. "We could have come back to life if you had let us." She turns away from him and drops into her car seat. She closes the door, starts the engine, and backs out onto the road.

Jack stands to watch his wife drive toward Harry, her car a red flash on the hillside.

He wonders about the dry heat and pale desert land-scapes of Arizona.

And, for the first time in months, he feels hungry.

TAKING STOCK

Sally Collins lies stretched out in the dental chair, her softly rounded belly and generous bosom gently rising and falling. Dr. Henry Jones and his assistant exchange a look, their eyebrows lifting higher above bright blue masks. Their patient has snoozed through a root canal. Henry pulls off his latex gloves and shoots them into the bin next to the sink. A tired sigh floats out of him. On his plod out of the room, he sneaks a final scan of Sally.

Oh, how he'd love to be rich.

When Sally first sashayed her hourglass figure and pearly teeth into his office, she had bowled him over so hard, he still hadn't found his footing. A rich man would have bowled her over right back. But since rich men's wives are stuck to them like wads of gum on the soles of their sneakers, those guys never need to protect their backsides from wifely spite. Henry snorts. No such luxury exists in his world. Estelle would sic a razor-toothed lawyer on his ass, and snatch his last dime.

He drops into his office chair and stares at the ceiling. There are days when he can hardly bear his life as a dentist, and this is one of them. For more than twenty years, he's crouched over wonky teeth and spongy gums, hardly daring to breath lest he get a nose full of stench. And for what? Not for riches, that's for sure.

He yearns for the past and the opportunity to correct this huge mistake. Even though he comes from a long line of dentists, he should have been an architect, and dreams every day of handsome buildings of his own creation. Look at how well he sculpts his patients' crowns and bridges. He understands artistry, symme-try, and the beauty of geometric harmony. He would have been a famous architect. The wealthy would have lined up to have him design their homes, as shown in those glossy interior design magazines. He'd be richer than a Frank Lloyd Wright if he'd followed his true dream.

He imagines himself on one of those big fancy boats, afloat in the middle of Lake Michigan, leaning back in his personally designed chair, facing the sun, his fishing rod on one side, a cold beer on the other.

Sally Collins' dusky voice breaks though his thoughts. "Thanks Doc, I didn't feel a thing." She's standing in his doorway, blond hair shining like a halo, peach cheeks flushed from her nap, her flowery dress so tight it looks like she might explode out of it.

He has to fight with his eyes to keep them off her curves. His mouth is watering. "Well, that's the way it's supposed to be," he manages to declare in his best dentist voice.

His assistant Maria calls from behind her. "Our next hour's just canceled."

"Must be fate," Sally says with a smile. "Okay if I come in for a few minutes?"

Without waiting for a reply, she breezes into his office and arranges herself in the chair next to his desk. He notes that her bare legs are pale and smooth. Her perfume—rich and spicy—causes a stir in his gonads. "Let's talk about corn," she says.

He wrestles with his eyes, forcing them to lodge on her face and not on the small triangle of space that appeared between the hem of her dress and her closed thighs when she first sat down; a mysterious space that likely leads to a view of her panties. He mops his fore-head with a Kleenex. "I'm all ears," he quips.

In full recline on his chaise longue, Henry watches Estelle toss two strip steaks onto their patio grill, her face set into hard lines. "There's no way anybody can guarantee an investment in corn," she pronounces, in that superior tone of hers that irritates him to no end.

"Well, the woman who *owns* the investment com-pany showed me the prospectus, legal documents that spell out the ten percent guaranteed minimum payoff. The key word being *guaranteed.*"

"Yeah, right," Estelle snorts. "Commodities are high risk. How can corn be guaranteed to grow?"

"And ten percent is the *minimum* payout. Could even hit two hundred percent, or more. All done and dusted within three months."

"I sure hope you don't plan to give this mystery woman a nickel of our money, such as it is."

"Don't worry, she won't get one nickel out of me," he mutters, wishing he dare tell his smart-ass wife that Sally got $25,000 out of him instead. He could envision the headlines that would follow in the *Bird Lake Daily* if he did. "Deranged Wife Takes Out Cornball Husband."

The payoff would come too late to save him.

Truth be told, Estelle is a woman not to be messed with. On their wedding night she told him, "If you ever cross me, just remember that you have to sleep some-time."

How could he forget that? Yet, he has never both-ered to devise a provisional plan explaining the future getting of his long dreamed-about boat to Estelle—a boat that he will have paid for with cash she never knew existed, his own secret stash. How had he expected to sneak that one past her and still manage to sleep nights?

"What's the matter?" Estelle is staring at him, her sharp blue eyes fastened on his. "You look pale."

He shrugs. "Just overworked, I guess."

She drops their steaks onto plates and hands one to him. "You need red meat," she declares, "and a glass or two of red wine." She slides open the patio door and stands back to let him in. She lands a kiss on his cheek as he steps into the house. "Don't worry Old Honeybun. We'll get you fixed up," she says gently.

His heart starts to soften, just like it always does whenever she acts this way. His Estelle. That is how he thinks of her. She waited tables to help put him through dental school, putting her own education on hold until he was set up in practice. She settled happily into the fancy house he always wanted. She let him design their traditional oak kitchen cabinets instead of putting in the modern Italian things she likes. She enjoys being a librarian, and loves reading travel books and describing all of the places she's dreamed of seeing but never has, because the money's not there. She loves him. What more could a man want?

His head flashes him pictures of Sally Collins' bare legs and voluptuous breasts. His gut jumps like a jack-in-the-box with its lid lifted. Under Estelle's watchful eyes, he sits at the head of the table sawing his steak like a man possessed.

Sally Collins reclines in a sunbathing pose, flat on her back with one knee slightly raised. If Henry could just think of an excuse to get up and walk around the dental chair, he would see right up her skirt. He tries to shush these ideas, but his cheeks heat up anyway.

"Good going, Doc," Sally purrs. "This looks perfect." She is admiring the crown that covers her root canal, holding up the hand mirror, turning her head back and forth, opening and closing her mouth. Her pink gums shine with health. "You're the greatest."

Without waiting for his go-ahead, Maria starts raising the back of the dental chair, lifting their patient into an upright position. Sally's sturdy bosom—a rosy cleavage that airs much of itself above a plunging neckline—demands his attention as it edges closer.

He catches Maria staring at him, her eyes narrowing in disapproval. Blushing like a fool, he jumps up and says, "After you've settled up at the front desk, will you stop into my office for a business minute, Sally?

Sally swings her legs around, giving him a glimpse of black satin underwear. "I'm all yours."

Maria's eyes are boring holes through him. She and Estelle are friends. They're always doing lunch together, talking about god-knows-what. Probably him. He wonders what she'll say to his wife about Sally. He should never have mentioned corn to Estelle.

His office is as chilly as a North Pole igloo; the air conditioning ramped up to freezing levels. Flopping into his chair, he sighs long and loud.

"What's up, Doc?" Sally plops down in the chair.

"I'm wondering how the corn deal is shaping up." Since he's just as interested in her shape this isn't entirely true.

"So far, so good," she bubbles. "In fact, most of my clients have added considerably to their initial investments."

"Really?"

"As you know, this could easily be a once in a lifetime opportunity."

"Well—"

"Don't tell me you're a worrier," she teases, gently poking his chest with a beautifully manicured fore-finger.

"Not a worrier exactly, just a good businessman."

"That's why you acted on your gut," she taps her stomach with both hands when she says this. "Believe me, Henry, not everyone has your kind of savvy."

He tries not to appear pleased, but his lips lift anyway. "I guess I'm pretty good at following my instincts."

"What else are you good at?" she murmurs.

He starts salivating like a starving dog eying a bowl of treats. Sally leans toward him, lips parted, eyes half closed. He swallows hard and touches her arm, which is soft and silky, praying he's reading her signs right. He'd like nothing more than to——

"It's almost six o'clock," snaps Maria from the door-way. "I need to lock up."

Sally winks at him and smooths down her skirt.

"Give us a minute, Maria," he says in his big boss voice.

"Okay," she replies, without moving an inch.

Sally's smile widens.

"I told you to give us a minute."

"And I said, okay," Maria answers, her voice defiant, her feet locked down.

Sally stares at him, her smile fixed in place. She's waiting to see how he'll respond to his brazen assistant, his busybody employee.

"Give us a minute in private," he roars.

"No need to shout," Maria retorts, before flouncing off in a huff.

He pictures her on the phone already, "Estelle, Henry is losing it over this sexpot Sally woman. He acts like he could do her right on his desk."

"Nobody can get one over on you, Henry," observes Sally, scanning him up one side and down the other.

He can't remember when he last felt so alive. His heart revs up and he hears his own voice saying, "I think I might as well double my investment with you."

She leans over his desk as he writes out the check, her breasts almost departing from their black lacy harness. His hands shake so much he can barely read his own writing.

Henry cannot—dare not—sleep. All night he has tried to force his eyes shut, but they refuse to do it. Estelle lies beside him emitting soft, regular breaths. Apparently, she has not been informed about his financial shenanigans, but he just can't tell for sure.

With a bit of luck he can pull this off. His wife has always trusted him with their finances, which is how he acquired his delicious secret stash in the first place. So long as Maria doesn't give her a reason to pry into things, he will have the $25,000 he'd just removed from their savings account put back, and the profits from the entire $50,000 investment rolled up and added into his secret stash. Estelle will be none the wiser.

Really, she should be grateful they have any savings at all; after all, he's had to build up his practice as well as build this marvelous house. That's when Estelle thought she could put the kibosh on him. "We can hardly pay for this house, let alone buy a damned boat," she'd complained, in that shrill I'm-so-fed-up tone of hers.

Henry's annoyance builds. He should be the one to complain. Because of her, he was forced to secret away his boat money.

He imagines catching fish with Sally. They're lying naked on the deck of his boat in the middle of Lake Michigan, its vast turquoise waters sparkling beneath clear azure skies. She is turning to face him, her plump breasts rolling softly against his chest.

Moonlight floods the room as he reaches for Estelle, his eyes tightly closed.

Henry stares at his bank statements. His and Estelle's joint savings account shows a $5,942 bank balance, all that remains of their life savings. His secret stash is reduced to $515.20. For the umpteenth time, he runs through the numbers. Even with a minor profit in his corn investment, there's no way he can lose. His ten percent guaranteed return will add up to a $5,000 profit.

But if 1984 turns into a spectacular year for corn growers (or is it a bad year that's needed so they can hike prices? He just can't remember) and he receives a hundred percent profit, he'll be $50,000 richer. A two hundred percent profit would lift him into six figures. In only three months!

Eyes closed, he leans back in his chair and envisions his future boat bobbing on his horizon. When he makes it big, he'll scoot Sally onboard. She'll wear a string bikini, a black one. He'll be in charge of the suntan lotion.

Maria raps on his open door. "Estelle is on the line," she shouts, like he's a mile away from her.

His shoulders slump. Everyone is acting weird lately, even his wife. She's becoming too much the happy camper for his liking. She's oozing with something he can't quite pin down, something altogether new. He taps his pen against the desk.

"What's wrong, Estelle?" he grumps down the phone line.

"Nothing's wrong, Honeybun," she says cheerfully. "I just want to let you know I'm heading out for dinner with an old friend tonight. There's leftover chicken in the fridge. I might be late getting in, so don't bother waiting up."

Henry's brain shoots out shock waves that leave him stultified. His mouth is open, but emits nothing.

"I'm late for a hair appointment," Estelle says, sounding a tiny bit exasperated. "I'll talk to you later."

For a long time Henry doesn't move. It takes a bellow from Maria to get him onto his feet and along the hall. His prepped patient is laid out like a corpse, hands folded across his chest and mouth agape. Henry pulls up his stool, his mind on Estelle, his heart thudding out its dismay. When he reaches for his mask, he smells a whiff of decay.

Estelle hasn't been home all night. Still in his brown and blue striped pajamas, Henry downs his coffee, grateful that it's Saturday and he doesn't have to go to work. He replays her phone message. "Hi sweetie. I've had a little too much wine so I'm staying with my friends tonight. I'll be home tomorrow afternoon, probably later in the day."

For the first time in his life, he fears losing her. He cannot imagine where she is, only that she has never done anything like this before. Now she's laid this whopper on him, like she's been secretly saving herself up to blindside him all along. Why? He's always been good to her, at least, so far as she knows.

He feels the rise of bile. His Estelle is with a man. Otherwise, she wouldn't be acting so damn secretive. Right? His heart thumps harder against his eardrums. Well, he'll be damned if he's going to sit around here all day waiting for her to show up.

He yanks his little black address book out of his desk's bottom drawer, and starts thumbing through it, coming across Sally Collins' phone number almost like magic. Before he can change his mind his fingers start dialing.

"Sally, are you free for lunch? Blue Sky Restaurant on the Lake? One o'clock?"

Sally doesn't speak. He hears George Michael's big hit "I Want Your Sex" playing in the background, and wonders if she too is in her pajamas (or smoldering neg-ligee), drinking coffee at her kitchen table. His hands are sweating and he's breathing like a jogger on an up-hill run. Finally, she says. "Okay Henry. See you there."

His legs threaten to wobble out from under him. He accidentally shouts, "Yes!"

But then, when he's hanging up the phone, a terrible question pops into his head, the one he's tried to ignore all along: Does Estelle know about the corn deal, and Sexpot Sally?

Like agent double-oh-seven, Henry sits at a corner table, peeking through tall spiky plants, checking out the Blue Sky diners. So far, he's found no familiar faces. At first he'd wondered what was wrong with him, choosing such a popular, busy restaurant for his tryst with Sally. Now, he's starting to believe that he pan-icked for no good reason. If need be, he'll simply tell Estelle that she was supposed to come along with him, to this restaurant, to meet Sally Collins and to learn about investing in commodities, or whatever else people invest their money in these days. (It's all like Chinese to him.) But, since she was missing in action, he was forced to come here without her. It's her own fault he's had to come on his own.

Besides, Estelle will eventually come to appreciate his financial planning, his savvy corn investment. She wants to see him succeed; she always has. Money softens the hardest of hearts, and he plans to make lots of it. Once it's rolling in, Estelle might even turn a blind eye to his rich man dalliances, like the one he plans to start today with Sally.

Between the stalks of a large fiddle-leaf fig plant, he catches sight of Sally bouncing across the restaurant floor, high heels clicking against the parquet. Men's eyes follow her, eager to see the lucky dog rich man who has snagged a woman like this. He wishes he could stand up and show himself off to them. Four weeks from now, after he's hit the financial jackpot, he will buy his new boat and moor it in front of this place. They might as well drool over that as well.

"Why Henry," Sally air kisses his cheeks, "you naughty boy."

The sound of his name gliding from her lips nudges at his groin. He senses a lift in his trousers. He feels like a teenager, all excited and dithery, testosterone shoot-ing through his veins. He quips, "Just remember that naughty boys look for bad girls." Then he raises one eyebrow and smiles rakishly.

"I'll keep that in mind," she murmurs.

The waiter appears, a bent old man with eyebrows grown like tufts of wild grass. His eyes sweep Sally, her length and breadth measured in one go. He passes Henry the wine list.

"Chardonnay, Sally? White wine doesn't stain teeth."

She nods, looking amused.

The waiter shuffles off on sad sack feet. That guy would have to own trillions of dollars before a woman like Sally would notice him.

"Henry, why have you asked me here?"

He thinks it is obvious, and is surprised by the question. He checks his silverware for spots lifting his fork and turning it toward the light. "What do you mean?"

"That is a wedding ring on your finger, right?"

"Yes, but—"

"You're not going to tell me that your wife doesn't understand you, are you?"

"I love my wife," he retorts.

"Well then, why are we here?" She is all business now. Gone is the seductive smile, the promise of an agenda like no other, the romp to beat all romps.

He can't say he wants revenge on Estelle, who was no doubt out on a dalliance last night and still hasn't come home. Donald Trump would never admit that, even if it were true. He decides to try flattery and a measure of truth. "You're a beautiful woman, Sally. What man could resist you?"

"You want the cake and the cookie too?"

"Can you blame me for wanting a taste of you?"

"Would your wife?"

The waiter is reaching over him to give Sally her wine. She's giving him the eye, flattering the old coot so that his day is made. Henry wonders if she is like this with every man. His stomach is tight and his ears feel warm.

"Why are you here, Sally?"

She shrugs. Her breasts practically rest on her place mat, begging for a good long ogle.

The waiter thrusts a menu at him.

"I'm starved," Sally sings.

She orders the lobster—the most expensive thing on the menu—and another Chardonnay to wash it down.

To offset her extravagance, Henry zeros in on the house hamburger—dubbed "Garbage Burger" since everything imaginable is on it—but remembers in time that his rich man façade does not allow for signs of stinginess. He orders the New York strip steak, extra rare.

"Would you like a nice red wine with your steak," asks the waiter, sounding a lot like his wife.

"Your house Merlot will do," Henry mutters, wondering if Estelle has arrived home yet.

Sally rests against the back of her chair, sipping her drink as she studies him. "So Henry, you're a married man who loves his wife, but you still like to have a bit on the side."

"I'd hardly call a woman like you a bit on the side."

"How many women have you had during your marriage?" she asks, smiling.

He weighs this carefully. A rich man would tell all, and Sally seems to think he is a bit of a catch, yet, there is a danger in blabbing too much. On the other hand, she's opened up the topic of sex.

"I've had one or two ladies along the way," he ventures, "None like you."

"Is that one, or is that two?"

In fact, there were three. Two were his former dental assistants, unhappily married women content with a glass of wine in his office and a hop onto the dental chair for a fast one before heading home on Friday nights. The other was a waitress who worked with Estelle when Henry was in dental school. She used to meet him between classes in her old VW van with flower decals all over it and a mattress in the back.

"You must know your way around a woman," Sally murmurs with heightened interest.

The waiter sets down Sally's lobster plate and fusses with the placement of her water glass. He heard what she said and his smirk tells Henry that he doesn't believe it for a minute.

Sally eats with a gusto that delights him, dunking each chunk of lobster into melted butter and adding a squeeze of lemon before raising it to her adorable open mouth. Estelle has a tendency to pick at her food, calorie counting like an adding machine. That's how she keeps that skinny, boyish figure her friends envy. It's because of her he can't keep his eyes off curvy women.

It's because of her he can't stop dreaming of what it must be like to run his hands over a roller coaster body like Sally's. It's all Estelle's fault really.

His wife's warning pushes itself into his head. "How can corn be guaranteed to grow?" This time Estelle's question lands in his ears, and a bout of nerves strikes. He pushes his cleaned-off plate away. "We need to talk about my investment," he says, carefully.

Sally's eyes dance. "Why Henry," she teases. "Is that a worried look?"

He feels shaky, and suspects he's as white as a toddler's tooth. "How can investments in corn be guaranteed?" he blusters. "How can you promise me a return on my money?"

"Henry," she says, serious now. "You have a legal contract. Would I lie to you?"

It occurs to him that he doesn't know. He doesn't even know if she'll pay for her root canal and porcelain crown, because his disorganized bookkeeper sent out his bills so late.

Sally is looking at her watch. "Jeez!" she cries. "We'll have to do this another time."

Henry's heart hits bottom.

Out of nowhere, the bill slides onto the table next to him. Henry makes a mental note. Next time he'll avoid this nosy waiter's station.

In the parking lot, they stand beside her car, a brand new 1987 Corvette, a polished-to-perfection bright yellow, with the twin-turbo option. Business must be good.

"Let's get together next week, Sally," he smiles, his confidence restored.

She plants a soft kiss on his cheek. "I'd like that," she whispers. "Next time it's on me." She slides her hips into the Corvette's driver's seat. He glimpses her shocking pink panties as her legs swing by.

He drives home like a lunatic, racing along twisting country roads, rolling through stop signs in Bird Lake Village, hoping that after her big night out, Estelle is in the mood for a very early bedtime.

In broad daylight, his Estelle lies in their bed out for the count like Sleeping Beauty. A flimsy red dress has been tossed onto the bedroom chair, a pair of spike-heeled sandals rest toe-to-toe on the floor. These things cannot belong to his wife. He blinks and squints across at them, wondering how they got here. His wife sighs deeply, her face sweetly innocent, like a child's.

He checks out their guest bedroom. No red dress wearer in there. He sticks his head into their third bedroom. Same result.

In the kitchen, he pours himself a large glass of white

wine and heads for his study. There's something scary about Estelle, something that makes his gut want to freeze. If he were a gambler, he might bet that Estelle knows what he's up to with Sally.

That creep Maria must have told her something was going on. The two of them were probably out on the town last night, two foolish, married women out on the prowl. He catches his breath. Lots of rich men are out looking for beautiful women in red dresses, especially beautiful married women who want to keep mum about their extramarital samplings. He releases his breath with a whoosh. Estelle has bought quite a few clothes lately. "For once in my life, I'd like some trendy, sassy stuff," she told him. That red dress is damned sassy, and those shoes, well, nothing gets sassier than those shoes.

At a loss over what to do now, he trudges into his study, sits down at his desk, and then jerks to attention. His private papers drawer is unlocked, its key lying on the desktop next to his expensive glass boat paper-weight. Flooded with fear, he yanks it open. His investment folder sits right where he left it. He opens it up with trembling hands. On top, Sally's gaudy red letterhead nearly blinds him. Copies of his bank transactions lie behind it. Everything is as it should be and yet nothing feels right.

Sweat sprouts on his brow. He locked that drawer. He knows he locked it. Surely she hasn't been snooping. Not his Estelle. He gulps his wine and holds the glass to his chest with both hands. She's had every opportunity. For starters, she gets home from work earlier than he does.

Henry sits frozen in his chair. Since the day they met he has trusted her completely, and now this. He envisions a razor-toothed attorney. How can he save his ass now? He'd better keep mum about this discovery and let Ms. Snoopy think she's not been found out. Once he gets the corn payoff from Sally, and gets their life savings back in place, he'll move his secret stash to a Swiss bank account (do people really do that?) and file for divorce before she can.

Pain rattles around his chest. He can't imagine why. After all, he hasn't loved Estelle for years.

Monday morning, Henry wakes up alone in the guest bed and listens intently to the quiet. Estelle is usually up first, banging around in the bathroom, or clashing about in the kitchen; making lots of noise is one of her more annoying habits.

She disappeared again all day yesterday, sneaking out of the house before he could catch her, leaving a note on the kitchen table that said, "Out shopping. Back late." He waited for her until midnight, sitting on the couch fuming, his imagination running amuck. Who was she with?

He was forced to give up his wait. A dentist needs his sleep. But, after the way she'd behaved—so out of character—he was determined to show her a thing or two. Which is why he moved into the guest room.

Yet now he'd love to hear her morning racket. His worry is mounting. He doesn't like what's happening to his life, which was easy and comfortable before Estelle started getting sassy. She has spoiled everything.

He tosses back the covers, dangles his legs over the edge of the bed, and sits still for a few minutes. The house contains not a peep of noise. Perhaps she has overslept.

His heart is flip-flopping as he opens the master bedroom door. The bed is unmade, which surprises him. Estelle is such a neat-freak she's been known to try and make the bed while he's still in it. The bathroom door is closed.

"Estelle" he shouts. "Are you in there?"

An unwelcome thought pops into his head. Maybe Estelle is dead. Maybe she thought she'd lost him to Sally, and stayed out for a final fling last night before doing the deed. Don't they say that the strong fall hardest? He shivers, afraid to push open the door. She could be hanging from the bathroom ceiling, or drowned in the bathtub, or sprawled out on the floor, overdosed from drugs gulped down in anguish.

"Estelle," he croaks. "Can I come in?"

He can't get hold of Sally. He's left three messages with her answering service and nobody has called him back. He would drive over to her business address if he knew where it was; her letterhead lists only a post office box. His heart pummels his ribcage.

"Hi Henry." Maria saunters in. "Guess who I saw on my drive to work?"

A sense of dread washes over him. "I've no clue," he says, irritated by the idea that she is setting him up.

"I saw Estelle. She was coming out of the 6th Street Diner with Sally."

His heart leaps so hard it hurts his eyes. He spins his chair around to face her. "Are you sure?"

Maria cannot hide a smile. "I didn't know they knew each other."

Neither did Henry. His brain is in a tangle.

"Cancel my appointments," he sputters. "I'm heading home."

His house looks unlived in. He's never noticed that before. Even as the sun shines down on it, the windows look dark as sunglasses; his cleverly carved front door looks like it belongs on a dungeon.

He left this morning believing that Estelle might be out on a run, despite her aversion to any form of exercise that creates sweat. "Joggers are so undignified," she liked to say, "Running about the streets, sweat flying, a look of agony etched onto their faces." Yet, this morning, after finding their bathroom empty, he wanted to believe that the new, sassy Estelle had joined them. Obviously, he had deceived himself.

He drags himself along the hall to his study, but crosses the floor to his desk in just two steps. He's panting like a marathon runner, and just as damp. Sally's prospectus is lying on the desktop—another red flag, another warning that all is not well.

He spies a business envelope from Sally Collins' Investments. He rips it open. It's a check made out in his name. It's the $5,000, the ten percent guaranteed payout on his investment. For a moment, relief gives him an enormous boost. He can hardly wait until Estelle sees that he was right to trust Sally.

But then he pictures the two of them together, coming out of the 6th Street Diner, and does not know what to make of that.

A slow dawning creeps up on him. Where is his $50,000? He was promised a ten percent return on his

$50,000. This check should be for $5,000 *plus* his $50,000. This check is $50,000 short.

His eyes start to lose focus. Sweat drenches his shirt. Was he guaranteed a ten percent return and nothing else? Has he given away $50,000 to get a *guaranteed* $5,000? He fans himself with the *Bird Lake Daily*, and totters into the kitchen for a bottle of wine. He needs to calm down and read the small print on the pro-spectus.

He bangs open the kitchen booze cupboard to reveal his stash of fine wines. His jaw drops. Propped up against a nice Chianti, is an 8"x10" glossy photo. He swallows hard and takes a step backward. Is that Sally and Estelle standing together on the deck of one of those big fancy boats, wearing short-shorts and halter-tops, arms wrapped around each other in a most undignified way? They're grinning like a pair of imbe-ciles. They look almost lovey-dovey.

He has to sit down when he sees that the boat is docked in front of the Blue Sky Restaurant. Yellow paint spells out its name: "Corn Flowers."

Is this supposed to be a joke?

He jumps up and snatches the photo off the shelf, then watches in dismay as another falls out from behind it. He picks it off the floor and collapses back into the chair at the kitchen table.

It takes him a minute or two of deep breathing before he dare take a look.

A shy young woman, a girl really, stands beside a white VW van with flower decals stuck all over it. She's thin and boyish. Her hair is light brown and cropped short. She wears no makeup. Nonetheless, he can see why he liked her. She was sweet and pretty, aside from that nose.

To calm the scramble in his brain, he opens the bottle of Chianti and pours himself a full glass. After gulping it down, he manages to look closer at this face from twenty years ago. He sees now that she was *very* young, and divinely innocent, this waitress who worked with Estelle.

He thinks her name was Laura.

She was barely eighteen when they used to have sex in the back of her van. He was twenty-six and married. But he had promised her his dentist's world. "When I graduate, I'll set up my practice, and we will live happily ever after." He snorts and attempts a sardonic smile. She knew he was married. He taught her a good lesson about trusting in the wrong people.

A second full glass of Chianti relaxes his shoulder muscles, a problem area for dentists. He goes for another refill and prepares himself to think. What is really going on here? He feels like he's supposed to put together a big jigsaw puzzle, something that will fit together just right, if he can only find that missing piece.

The afternoon sun filters through their kitchen blinds and falls across the photo, highlighting Laura's face. His eyes are trying to tell him something. He turns the picture over. "I've grown up, Henry," is scrawled across the back.

Henry clasps his chest. Air leaves his lungs. He picks up the boat photo and gawks at Sally's grinning face— so much like Laura's, aside from that pert nose, an apparent testament to the Joy of Plastic Surgery.

He pictures sassy blond Sally flaunting her curves at him, grown so luscious over the past twenty years, and thinks of how he pursued her all summer.

His Estelle will have known all along.

He sees the white flowered VW van, the old mattress, and the girl who used to look at him with pure adoration. Now she drives a brand new top-of-the-line yellow Corvette. She owns her own company. She is doing whatever she wants to do, and not just dreaming about it.

The Chianti bottle is empty. He reaches for another.

He can already smell Estelle's razor-toothed lawyer —a Dickensian character awash in Old Spice—and fights the urge to put his hands over his ass.

Sally has whipped his money out from under him. She has stolen his wife. She has stolen from him his comfortable dentist life. She even has his goddamn boat, no doubt purchased with his $50,000.

He lets out a scream.

A woman like that won't even pay for her root canal and porcelain crown.

DUNE BUG

Azure seas lap against golden sand dunes that undulate along the shoreline like a cluster of double chins, sharp grasses grown on them like whiskers. From within their midst, a newborn baby wails. Hunched in a remote dip, a wide-eyed girl of fifteen presses the child to her. Her teenage boyfriend kneels beside them holding a white beach towel, and a small red cooler filled with sun-warmed seawater.

They had once made love amongst these dunes. Might even have been right here, Dave thinks. They had lain naked on this same blanket, red tartan against yellow sand, not knowing then that they were making this child.

He watches Ellen gently rinsing the last of her blood from their baby's toes. A thrill scurries up his back. He can hardly wait to show off his beautiful boy.

"I'm glad he decided to be born here, out in the sunshine," Ellen says, almost to herself, wrapping her son in the towel. "It makes him special."

On shaky feet they peek out of their cocoon to survey the new lay of the land. From one end to the other, the beach looks deserted.

"After this, we can face anything together," Dave says.

Her head shakes no, but her mouth says, "Yes."

"Now I just have to find a decent job."

"You're sixteen, Dave. You don't even have a high school diploma yet."

"I'll stay in school and work nights and weekends, or whatever." He has never failed at anything, and he's not about to start now.

Ellen's entire body hurts, especially her private parts —made not so private now. Her cheeks flush. The pain and exposure of giving birth has made her feel humiliated and angry.

Her friends told her she would forget the pain; as if they know anything about having a baby. While she was giving birth to her son, they were in class preparing for college. What do they know about anything at all?

Her mother's voice echoes in her ears. "Who do you think will *not* go to college now, Ellen? You or Dave?"

Dave would graduate with the class of '86, one year ahead of her. They both knew that he was primed for college and a career in business. No matter what he says now, Ellen bets he'll get there one way or another.

Dave holds the baby against his chest with one big clumsy hand, and helps her sit back down on the blanket with the other. "We'll just wait here until you're ready to head out," he says, his face anxious. "No rush, Ellen. It's a beautiful day."

She had decided to skip school this morning; Dave was against it. "It's too close to your due date," he warned.

"I've a week to go," she said. "Besides, I hate school on Mondays." She had loved school before she got pregnant, before she became the center of attention for all the wrong reasons. She wants to be a lawyer.

She lifts her face to the sun and takes in the vastness of the sky and ocean, and the world. The weight of her lost freedom grows; the sense of her own smallness and insignificance builds.

Her baby whimpers.

She wonders how Dave thinks they will both go to

school, and go to work, and also take care of their baby while he saves for college. "Where will we live, do you think?" she says.

They've talked about this a thousand times before; but until today, nothing they discussed ever seemed real. She thinks that Dave doesn't get what has happened to them. And to their baby.

Dave looks to the horizon, where the water meets the sky in a dark blue line that appears drawn on with crayon. "We'll find an apartment, somewhere near school," he says with confidence.

She wants to slap him. "Who will watch the baby while we go to school?"

Her own mother had said that she wouldn't do it. "I've raised kids my whole life," she cried. "Don't forget, I come from a family of ten and I was the oldest." She wiped her eyes with her hands and took a deep breath. "I raised my parents' kids, and then my own kids, and I can't start raising yours."

The baby's fingers wrap tighter around Ellen's forefinger.

"I could ask my mom to watch him, I suppose," Dave says, as if they have another option.

The baby wails.

Ellen unbuttons her shirt. The school nurse talked to her about breast feeding. "It's the best thing you can give your baby," she advised. "It's the best start in life."

Ellen thinks now that the best start in life for a child would be two good parents with jobs and cars and a home to live in.

The baby starts suckling with surprising ferocity. Ellen winces in pain. Nobody warned her about this.

Fatigue is threatening to overwhelm her. She wants to lie down in a clean bed and sleep for as long as she likes and wake up to her old life.

Her mother's voice shows up again. "Don't plan to get a good night's sleep once the baby is born. Not for six months, at least."

Dave watches the baby with love-dazzled eyes. "What should we call him?" he asks, as if that was their biggest problem.

She fights to keep calm "I still like Ian. Don't you?"

"Now that I've seen him, I don't know if he really is an Ian." Dave smiles, shyly. "He looks more like a David to me."

"David the Second?" She manages a smile. "Okay."

Dave's smile widens. "Wait until we show up at the hospital with David the Second, our cute little dune bug."

"I think that's supposed to be June bug."

"Whatever." His eyes redden. "Everyone is going to love him, Ellen."

He cannot imagine that this won't be true. For starters, his mother will melt at the sight of her first grandchild, and that's all he'll need to get on with his life.

Ellen leans her head back against the warm dune. She doubts very much that Dave's mom will want to babysit her life away, any more than her own mother does. Dave's mom has a job in real estate, and has spent years building her client base. She won't likely give that up. "It's getting hot now," she says, trying to keep her eyes open.

"It's a good thing we went to all of those childbirth classes," Dave bubbles. "Who knew we would end up having to do this on our own?"

Dave had insisted they take every single class offered. "You never know," he said, "I might have to deliver the baby myself. It has been known to happen."

She never believed that it would. In fact, she never really believed that a child was growing inside of her. Instead, she just drifted along in a dream, imagining a cute house, and a yard with a swing, and her new husband, Dave, who would miraculously bring home a decent pay check each week. That is what made her pregnancy bearable.

Ellen feels awash in grief, and wonders if this is just the postpartum blues that she heard about.

"I think I might have died of shock if we'd not seen those videos on what it's like delivering a baby," she says, tears on the rise.

David the Second has fallen asleep at her breast. He has rosy cheeks and a puff of black hair. She passes him to his father and buttons herself up. She says, "I think we should get off the beach while I can still manage it."

He pushes himself onto his feet. "We'll just take it slow."

Dave's eyes shine with pride. He carries his towel-wrapped son on one arm, and encircles Ellen's back with the other. She thinks he looks as if he owns them both, and clings tighter to her red tartan blanket. Everything else she brought with her today has been left behind in the sand.

To avoid climbing the dunes, they walk along the water's edge. Miniature waves wash over their feet; seagulls screech overhead. In a fog of pain and weariness, Ellen trudges toward her future.

When they reach the car, Dave looks back across the beach to see how far they've come. Ellen watches him from the passenger seat. She holds onto her baby, and waits.

BRIDGEWORK

When cousin Jennifer Blythe peeked around the curtains and cried, "Wow! It's snowing real bad," everyone left the party early. Norah didn't blame them. She would have done the same. As their houseful of family and friends lined up for coats and leftover cake, she looked for Mike's face, but he wasn't there. Standing alone at the door, saying awkward goodbyes, she realized Brenda was missing as well. Yet her car sat under the neighbor's streetlight, waiting to take her home.

"Jingle Bells" played loudly as the front door closed and Norah began her reluctant trek up the stairs. She thought that even a man like Mike had his limits, even he couldn't do *this*.

But while hovering outside the door of their seclud-ed attic guest room she heard the bed creak, as if he was turning over. Sometimes he liked to make a real production of that, exaggerating the effort it took for a 6-foot 2-inch, 225-pound man to make a drastic change in position. When they were in college, he would toss around so much their old mattress would bounce her about like a big rag doll. They used to laugh and hug and end up in a tangle of arms and legs.

She eased the door open and stared inside. Her eyes at first refused to see; but her gut, always more honest, shot searing pain along barbed wire nerves.

Mike and Brenda were so busy with each other they didn't know she was there. They writhed on Norah's carefully chosen duvet, grunting and grasping at each other like they belonged in an X-rated movie, far too busy to notice their audience. They reeked of her own mulled wine.

Norah snatched Brenda from behind. She dragged her off Mike by her hair, dumping her onto the floor where she lay naked, arms and hands working to cover her breasts and crotch.

"We were roommates in college." Norah's heart thumped wildly. "You know me." It was all she could think of to say.

Mike pulled the covers up to his chin like a shy, wide-eyed girl. "Wait Baby, wait," he pleaded.

But Norah could not wait anymore.

Brenda's clothes lay in a pile on the floor. With a furious strength, Norah hoisted up the window in one move and flung everything out, decorating snow-covered trees with Brenda's flimsy underwear and pink dress.

"Don't," whimpered Brenda.

Norah picked up Brenda's purse and sent it flying into the yard, its contents scattering across a huge swath behind the house. Shoes followed.

Brenda cowered under the blanket she found draped off the end of the bed. Norah yanked her to her feet and headed toward the stairs.

Mike still clung onto the sheets, seeking protection from them against Norah's fury. He pulled them around him like a toga and struggled to stand. "Norah, don't do this."

"Don't you dare defend her."

Brenda raised her arms to her head, trying to save her hair from tearing out at the roots as Norah swung her around. "Get off me," she squawked.

"You ain't seen nuthin' yet." Norah marched her down the stairs, for the first time in her life grateful for her bigness and strength. She dragged Brenda along the back hall, opened the back door and threw her onto the steps.

Brenda begged, "I'll freeze out here. Mike, get my clothes. Help me!"

Mike stood his ground, knowing that if he stepped outside, Norah would lock him out too.

Under their red, green and gold Christmas flood-lights, as if on stage, Brenda climbed partway up a tree, legs spread wide, tiny breasts freezing in the cold, reaching for her pink dress. She sobbed and shook as she pulled on damp, snowy clothes and searched the ground for her car keys, house keys, wallet and purse.

"Here kitty, kitty, kitty. Come get your coat, kitty, kitty." Norah had never known such rage existed in her. She did not care that their neighbors peeked from darkened windows, did not care that Brenda could die, did not care about anything but exacting revenge. She had to see them both suffer right now, lest the pain of their unbearable betrayal kill her, leaving them un-scathed.

"Jesus! She could die out there Norah."

"Go save her then."

"Her car had better start right up."

"Who cares?"

She watched Brenda skitter down the driveway on her way to the street, half dressed, shoeless, her purse hanging open.

"Drive carefully," Norah shouted, tossing out her coat, "and stay warm." She slammed the door shut with a flourish and stomped into the kitchen.

Mike stayed on her heels, keeping her in sight. "Jesus, you're a damned harsh woman, Norah. Damned harsh."

Norah swung around to face him. "You're calling *me* a harsh woman?"

He raised up his hands as if to fend her off. "Calm down, Norah."

On the top of the stove, a pan of hot mulled wine perfumed the air. She lifted it up in both hands, the way a tennis player might grasp her racket in preparation for a strong backhand. She yelled, "For the record: *Brenda* is a harsh woman," and flung the contents across the room at him.

Mike caught a splash right across his cheek. He screamed in shock and covered his face with his hands. His sheet toga dropped to the floor. "You're fucking nuts!"

Norah threw the last of the wine at him, feeling sorry that it had cooled somewhat.

"If I'm nuts, what does that make *you?*" she steamed. "You invited Brenda to this party knowing that I didn't want her around anymore. And then you're in bed with her upstairs with me and everyone else downstairs. If that's not nuts, I don't know what is."

Mike lurched toward her, "I'm not putting up with this."

Norah held the pan higher. "Don't even think about it," she said. "You've done enough damage for one night."

He picked his toga sheet off the floor and wrapped it around his body lest she aim for specific targets.

"Look at my face," he shouted.

She noted a pinkish stripe and gave a shrug.

"You could have scarred me for life."

"Oh boy! Brenda might not like you then."

He tightened up his toga and headed toward the stairs.

"Don't think you're living here with me after this, Mike."

"You couldn't pay me to live here now."

"Have fun at your mother's."

"I'm going to catch up with Brenda to see if she's all right," he shouted. "If she's found dead out there, we'll both be up for murder."

Norah sat opposite Jennifer Blythe in a shocking pink vinyl booth in the small diner owned by Jennifer. Nobody knew how she had managed to buy a restaurant. But it seemed best not to ask.

Jennifer was the only member of Norah's family to have ever spent time in prison. In her early twenties she had been a mail carrier, and stood accused of interfering with the United States mail after losing a multitude of envelopes containing cash and checks, and packages filled with expensive, insured items.

She had been surprised when Jennifer phoned to invite her to lunch. Had she not been so discombobulated, she would have found a way to refuse.

"I could have ended up in prison over those two," Norah said between bites of hamburger. "But even a preacher would have heaved Brenda out the door, snow or no snow."

"I never really minded prison," Jennifer mused. "You'd be surprised at how much you learn in there." She was beautiful and big, like Norah, almost six feet tall and a solid one-eighty. Her don't-mess-with-me attitude ensured that nobody did.

"Well, I'd rather not find out first hand what prison is like."

"I would never have imagined Mike with Brenda," Jennifer waved her empty coffee cup at a sturdy, orange-haired waitress who immediately headed over. "Brenda is such a weedy little thing. He seems to like more substantial women. Like you."

"Brenda threw herself at him and he couldn't say no, as usual."

Norah never imagined she would be sitting here with Jennifer like they were friends as well as cousins. She'd always tried to avoid Jennifer. Even Mike once said, "She is one big scary broad. I wouldn't put any-thing past her." Norah had only invited Jennifer to their holiday party because she'd felt a sudden burst of Christmas spirit after they ran into each other at the mall.

"Well Cuz," Jennifer shook her head, her mouth pulled into a tight line "I wish I'd known the bastard was up to his old tricks."

"If you hadn't looked out of the window and warn-ed everyone about the snow storm, I might never have found out."

"That's true."

Norah shrugged. "My husband is a womanizer. There's nothing I can do to change that."

"That's true too. All you can do is even up the score."

Warnings darted around Norah's gut. "No good comes from that stuff, Jennifer."

"You might be surprised."

Neither of them spoke. The waitress began removing their empty plates. She refilled water glasses and told them about today's desserts. Laughter burst out of a young couple sitting close together at the counter.

Norah's anger flared. "I don't know if I can ever forget seeing the two of them in my guest bed going at it like rabbits. I was downstairs doing the perfect hostess thing; laughing, joking, filling up glasses and clearing away plates for people."

"You've thrown him out already, right?"

"Right."

"Maybe you have to let him crawl back in." Jennifer smiled at her knowingly.

"Well," Norah hesitated. "I suppose I could." She stared across the table at Jennifer.

Jennifer's eyes regarded Norah from beneath lowered lids. "You've always been a dark horse, Cuz."

Mike stood at the back door bearing gifts: a dozen red roses and a gift basket filled with Godiva chocolates, which, Norah noted, included his own personal favorite, caramel pecan bark.

"Jennifer called me clear out of the blue," he blurted. "She thought you might be willing to talk." He raised the basket of chocolates as if tempting a dog with a few meaty bones.

She swallowed the urge to close the door on him. "I don't know, Mike——"

"I'm sorry for what I did."

"This isn't the first time you've been sorry."

"You know that even before Brenda got divorced she was coming onto me. She's not even my type, but I'd been drinking and I was flattered."

"You wouldn't put up with me if I'd done this with a friend of yours."

He hung his head. "I'll never cross you again, Norah. I promise."

She watched him squirm. After so many years, he had perfected his technique.

"You'd be wise not to cross me again," she said, opening the door wider.

There was a strut to his step when he crossed the threshold. "You won't be sorry, Sweetheart."

She hid her cringe when he touched her arm.

At the kitchen counter she plugged in the tea kettle and plunked down the French press coffee pot. "Where have you been staying?"

He hesitated. "My brother Ed's place."

"I thought you were staying with Brenda."

"I would never do that."

"You went there after I threw you out."

"I didn't stay though, Norah. I wouldn't want to give Brenda the wrong idea about me."

In that case, Norah thought, Mike had certainly given *her* the wrong idea about Brenda. Because from what she'd seen the other night, he had appeared to be quite at home with their X-rated crap.

"Please let me move back in, Norah."

She pretended to give this a long think. Mike edged the chocolate basket closer to her across the table.

She plastered on a wan smile. "You can stay in the guest room. We'll see how we go from there."

Mike beamed. "You got it, Babe."

He reached across the table and lifted the caramel pecan bark out of the basket. "Come on Norah," he pointed to the truffles. "Dig in."

Jennifer and Norah watched Brenda's house from the end of her street. The few houses around them were unlit. There were no street lights. With the car's head-lights switched off, they could barely see a foot in front of them.

Norah's doubts bubbled to the surface. "What if Brenda replies to that email."

"She won't. You wrote it from Mike's computer, so she'll believe that Mike sent it to her. She'll believe that she is not to write back to him in case you find it. And she's been told to stay off her cell phone."

"A woman like her ... she might want to have me find her letter on his computer."

"She won't dare. Not after what you did to her the other night."

"What if she doesn't want to go out tonight? She might not want to meet up with him again."

"She'll go all right. She would like nothing better than revenge, to stick it to you behind your back."

"What if Mike wakes up while I'm gone? He'll wonder why I took his car."

"You have to stop worrying, Norah," Jennifer hissed. "I thought you had more balls."

"I'm not sure about this, and I don't want to get caught."

Jennifer took a slow deep breath, as though to stabilize the minuscule amount of her patience that remained. "Well, she's your nasty friend, and your husband's tacky bitch. Do what you want."

Images of Brenda straddling Mike, her small breasts bouncing, his hands groping, began to blast through Norah. She could still smell the stench of her own mulled wine on their breath.

"I'm not backing out now."

"Good." Jennifer nodded her approval. "I've always said we're more alike than you think."

Norah felt a twinge of unease.

"Did you make sure he drank enough booze tonight, Cuz?"

"I did what you told me. He thought I was warming up to him. He didn't catch on to the fact that his drinks were spiked, and my gin and tonics had no gin in them. He was in bed before ten. I checked before I left, and he was totally zonked out."

Norah grinned. "Here she comes."

Brenda was slowly backing her car out of her drive-way.

"You were right," Norah felt breathless with fury. "She thinks she's on her way to a clandestine meeting with Mike. She *does* want to keep on sticking it to me behind my back."

"I just don't know how she can stand to live out here," Jennifer sniffed. "Talk about the boonies."

They waited until Brenda turned left at the corner before turning on their headlights and starting after her. For two miles they trailed along behind her, keeping their distance.

"She's probably wondering who we are and why we are on the road at midnight."

Jennifer laughed. "I bet she thinks it's Mike behind her."

As they neared the bridge, Norah moved in closer.

Brenda began slowing down.

"She *does* think it's Mike following her," Jennifer snorted. "Pull alongside her. Hurry!"

Norah felt a strong stab of fear. A warning. She wished she had time to think.

"Hurry up," Jennifer yelled. "Pull alongside her. *Now!*"

Norah nudged Mike's steering wheel in the direction of Brenda's car.

"Watch this." Jennifer switched on the flashlight, and pointed its beam at Brenda's face.

Brenda turned toward them. She was smiling.

In a blaze of fury, Norah swerved Mike's car even closer to Brenda's vehicle. Their side mirrors scraped.

"Let's show her what Mike really looks like." Jennifer shone the flashlight right into Norah's face.

"Stop it, Jennifer!"

Jennifer swung the beam back onto Brenda. "I bet she's not smiling now."

Brenda gaped at Norah, forgetting to watch where she was going. When she crashed through the rail, Jennifer sang, "There she goes: Thelma without her Louise."

Norah was pouring her morning coffee when Mike wandered into the kitchen. She felt more rested than she had in years. Jennifer had been right. Going on the offense was key to good mental health. She never would have thought she had it in her.

She handed Mike a coffee. "I was grading papers until about one. I hope I didn't wake you when I came upstairs."

"I can't hear a thing in that guest room. It's like a morgue up there." He reached for her knee. She swatted his hand away.

The doorbell rang.

"Who can that be?" Norah carried her mug to the door in shaking hands.

Mike looked up from his newspaper as Norah walked back in with two official looking men in dark suits.

"Mike, this is Detective Braun and Detective White. They want to talk to us."

Mike's eyebrows shot up. "About what?"

"A car went off the Dixon Bridge last night, Mr. Schwartz. It was driven by a friend of yours. Brenda Jessup."

Mike gasped and dropped his newspaper. "Is she all right?"

Norah sat down suddenly, as if the shock was too much for her.

"Where exactly were you last night, Mr. Schwartz?" Detective Braun kept his eyes on Mike's face.

"I was right here."

Detective White turned to Norah. "Is this true?"

Norah put on a bewildered look. "You told me you were out with your brother until after midnight."

Mike stared at her. "I didn't say that. What's going on?"

"Your car was seen out in Dixon last night," said Detective Braun. "Your license plate number was called in."

Norah felt like she was slowly sinking. Jennifer should have given her more training to prepare her for the aftermath.

"What time did this happen?" Mike directed his question to Detective Braun, but his eyes were fixed on Norah.

"If Mike says he was in bed, he was in bed," she said, without conviction.

"What about you, Ms. Schwartz?" Detective White asked. "Where were *you* last night?"

Norah's heart lurched and she fought down panic. "I was grading papers until midnight. Right here at the kitchen table."

"I can't vouch for that," Mike declared. "Like I said, I was in bed by nine-thirty."

The air before Norah was starting to look foggy. "Well, I can't vouch for you either, Mike."

The detectives exchanged a quizzical look.

"Well, we'll know soon enough," said Detective White.

"What do you mean?" Mike asked.

"Brenda Jessup is in intensive care right now, but she's expected to recover."

"Good," Mike said. "Then I don't have to worry."

Norah was struggling to hide her shock. She felt doomed. Jennifer had flooded her face with light so that Brenda could see who was running her off the bridge in Mike's car. She realized now that Jennifer would have been hidden from Brenda's view, sitting behind the light, in the passenger seat, in the dark.

Even so, Jennifer was there. They were both guilty.

She cannot imagine who could have seen Mike's car and called in his license number. The roads had been dark and deserted. Nobody had been watching them.

"We'll be in touch," said Detective Braun, as Norah closed the door behind them.

Mike and Norah faced each other.

"Your car is in the driveway, Mike. They'll be looking it over, checking it out."

"I've nothing more to say to you," he said, walking toward the stairs.

In his attic bedroom Mike snatched up his cell phone and quickly dialed a number. It rang four times before she picked it up. He couldn't help smiling about that. He liked a woman who wouldn't let any man own her —at least, at first.

"Hey Mike," she said in that cool, dusty voice of hers.

He could hardly contain his glee. "It's all worked out," he said. "Believe it or not, Brenda survived. But who cares? The two of us are in the clear. All we need now is for you to tell them that Norah went out last night, and that you were secretly up here in the guest room getting it on with me."

Her laugh, low and guttural, thrilled him. "Poor Norah," Jennifer drawled. "She always thought she was better than me. She didn't even invite me to her wedding."

EASTER IN DORSET

Gertrude and Archibald Bellamy sip their tea in the hotel's airy breakfast room. "This corner table gives us the best view in the house," she chirps, surveying the diners as if from a perch. She straightens her brown wool trousers and smooths her fine knit cardigan, admiring the way the light from the window catches her diamond and emerald ring.

"Quite right," says Archie, in the clipped English accent last heard on World War II newsreels. "And we've certainly seen a few frightful sights."

He's looking old now, Gertrude thinks, glancing at his neck, a crumple of folds; and his mouth, faded and weak. They've been married forty-four years. Just looking at him brings on fatigue. "Well," she sighs, "I expected to find a better class of people in a four star hotel. Especially in Dorset, over Easter."

She studies the unwitting diners, all dressed in casual clothes, laughing and talking with abandon. Who do they think they are?

Archie has ordered another pot of tea. He pours her a fresh cup before returning to *The Times*. She pictures him as her dashing young man and stifles a sob.

Their few friends are gone now; although, truth be told, she'd secretly felt relieved when the last one died. She'd harbored the hope that she and Archie could relax now that their world had somehow opened up.

"Where does one go these days to find like-minded people?" says Archie, as if speaking to no one in particular.

A smiling red headed woman strides into the room, tall, late forties, attractive, exuding a confidence that Gertrude finds quite irritating. With her is a handsome younger man with long flowing hair and black clothes. They sit at the next table.

Gertrude nudges Archibald, who is gazing blank-faced through the windows as if he doesn't have a moving part in his head. "Look at the odd couple next door," she says, tipping her head in their direction. "She certainly robbed the cradle."

The redhead's back straightens and her cheeks burn. Gertrude feels a pang of shame. She never used to speak so unkindly.

The odd couple leans toward each other, menus in hand. "What are you having, Maggie?" The young man's eyes shine; his smile is mushy. He looks like he's in his mid-thirties and appears to be completely smitten.

"How amusing," says Gertrude, feeling strangely stung.

"He's American," Archie speaks a bit too loudly, "That's how you used to sound, Gertie." He remembers meeting her in the Chicago Art Institute all those years ago. What a beauty, he thought. She was eighteen years old, on her last high school trip to the city. It was his first visit to America, and he fell in love.

Gertrude watches him stirring his tea. Her father used to stir his coffee with that same intensity every morning, before toiling his life away in the fields of their modest farm.

Her head fills with images of her tiny hometown: the dilapidated houses planted where they landed like rolled dice, paint bubbling from wood siding like foam on waves, rickety screen doors front and back, stiff windows, creaking floors, drab yards surrounded by chain link fences, the long dirt roads deeply rutted. Their Heinz 57 dog, Buster, would dig up the few flowers that struggled through their backyard's dirt each spring. Her eyes squeeze shut at the memory.

"I still sound American," she says with annoyance.

Archie smiles. "More mid-Atlantic now, Darling."

Gertrude looks over at Handsome Boy and Maggie, wondering what has brought them to England.

Maggie says to the waiter, "One full English please, and lots of coffee."

"She sounds mid-Atlantic too, although more English than American," Archie observes, laying aside his newspaper. "They're like us, one from each side of the Pond."

"They are hardly like us," Gertrude snips, before turning her attention back to their table.

Maggie is smiling at her young suitor like she won first prize in a raffle and is now set for life. "Do you suppose they are nouveau riche, Michael?" she says sweetly, wanting to give Gertrude an earful in return.

"There's a lot of that going around," Michael responds, making sure his voice carries.

Gertrude feels awed by Maggie's audacity. "How old do you think she is?" she stage whispers.

Archie raises his eyebrows. "Do you suppose they're married, Gertie?"

"I hope not."

Maggie rests her chin on her left hand. Her wedding ring flashes. "Jealousy is *sooooo* unbecoming," she says innocently. "Don't you agree, Michael?"

"It's a shameful thing," Michael responds, his face solemn as a mortician's.

Gertrude realizes that Maggie and Michael have never even bothered to look across at her. She is not sure if their responses to her taunts are imagined or coincidental. She bristles with annoyance. "That woman thinks she's rather special." Then she laughs uproariously, attracting attention and mortifying herself.

Archibald nods his head and guffaws like an old army general. She thinks he looks more like a pompous aristocrat with his country tweeds and British green tie.

"King Edward and Mrs. Simpson!" Maggie declares excitedly, as though answering a pub quiz question with the winning answer.

"Mr. and Mrs. Bucket," Michael deadpans. He pronounces it Boo-kay, like on the TV show *Keeping Up Appearances*.

Gertrude's heart starts doing gymnastics. She hates these people. Hates them! They walk in here with their casual airs and lowbrow wit thinking they can get the better of their betters. She motions to Archibald to get to his feet. Leading the way, she sweeps past the odd couple and their amused smiles. They look so happy, she thinks. And they have no right.

Maggie watches them leave, her smile fading.

"You're gorgeous Maggie. *That's* what annoyed her."

"You're gorgeous, Michael—and young. That's what annoyed her."

He laughs and grabs her hand. "Let's finish breakfast and get rolling."

In the hotel's car park they see Archibald standing by the open door of a sleek black Jaguar. Gertrude is nowhere in sight.

Maggie groans. "We should have known they'd have a Jag." Michael spreads the map out on the bonnet of their rental car, a mid-size blue box. She nudges him. "Those two think they're the bees knees."

Gertrude's voice reaches them. "Sounds like a Northern English accent," she says with a touch of disdain.

Maggie's heart starts to pound. She's transported back to the coal mines and slag heaps of her youth, and the upright, hard-worked coal mining families, like her own.

"Sounds like a Midwest American accent," Michael

muses, stroking his chin, his eyes on the clouds. "Probably some truck-stop town with dirt roads."

Maggie starts to laugh. "You're good," she whispers.

After a chilly walk along the Jurassic beach, and a tour of Lyme Regis, Maggie and Michael take off their warm coats and settle down for tea in the window of a quaint, traditional English teashop. Michael picks up another scone spread with strawberry preserves and Devonshire cream. "We should learn how to make these."

Maggie stirs her tea in slow motion. No matter how she tries, she can't brush away this morning's incident with that snooty couple. What was it that made them so mean spirited? Mind you, she hadn't been much better. Snooty people like that always brought out the worst in her.

"Don't let them get to you, Maggie."

"How did you know I was thinking of them?"

"They've hurt you with their spite."

She remembers herself at eighteen, dating a man with a private education and a posh accent—though where he got it from she could not imagine, since he'd grown up in a town five miles away from her village. When she met his parents they had tried to avoid shaking her hand, as if she was contaminated with something vile. After an awkward high tea, she had imagined them bleaching the dishes she had used, and disinfecting her seat. (And this is where she always has to squeeze her eyes shut.) On her way out of their house, she had thanked them for their hospitality.

"I hope we don't run into them again," she says, her stomach in a roil.

Dark clouds gather and rain sprinkles their windshield as they set off for their hotel. Maggie drives carefully along narrow winding roads, windscreen wipers flying as larger drops begin to spatter loudly against the glass.

"I might as well have driven both ways," Michael grumps. "The scenery is obliterated."

"I'll be glad to eat dinner in front of the hotel's fireplace tonight," she shivers. "If we're lucky, Mr. & Mrs. Snooty won't be there."

She slows down for an upcoming S-bend, taking care to stay tight to the left between beautiful high hedgerows. Ahead of them, a black vehicle sits pulled off to the side, its bonnet raised.

Michael leans forward and peers ahead. "Is that who I think it is?"

"Good grief," Maggie groans. "Now what?"

"Do whatever feels right for you."

Maggie drives toward the Jag, her head face-forward and her eyes pointed sideways so as to see what is going on. His head beneath the bonnet, Archie leans on his hands and stares down at the engine. Gertrude stands beside him trying to cover her head with a newspaper buffeted by high winds. They are soaked to the skin.

"Jeez!" says Michael. "I wonder if they have a cell phone between them."

Gertrude and Archie suddenly look over, aware that help might have stumbled upon them. Gertrude looks straight at Maggie, the driver, her face at first hopeful.

A pang of guilt and a spike of anger cause Maggie to avert her eyes. Why should she care what happens to them? They would leave her by the side of the road, no question. She could drown for all they'd care.

She drives slowly past them through a very large puddle, making sure she doesn't send a tidal wave their way. After all, she isn't completely heartless.

Michael stays silent.

"Well, say something," she snaps when they've rounded the bend.

"Don't take it out on me," he snaps back.

The rain is falling harder, almost drowning out his voice.

"Why should I care about those two awful people, Michael?"

"Do you think this really is about them?"

Maggie swings the car into a lay-by and slams on the brakes. "Don't start with me."

"I think maybe *you're* starting with you, Maggie."

Maggie pictures herself as a small child slowly discovering that she might never be deemed good enough. She was filled with grand ideas. Yet, when she'd said she wanted to be a scientist, her own parents had laughed. "That's not for the likes of us," they said. Even now, Maggie shrivels up at the thought of it.

"Maggie?"

"All *right*, Michael! I'll go back and get them." She's acting like a brat, but can't seem to stop.

Gertrude and Archibald stand in the rain, huddled together across from the Jaguar, their newspaper umbrella long abandoned. They appear so vulnerable Maggie's annoyance starts to unravel.

"It's too dangerous to sit in a car on a tight curve, on this narrow road," said Michael, telling her the obvious.

"Hello there," Maggie shouts, trying to sound cheerful. "Can we give you a lift?"

Archie and Gertrude exchange wary looks. "Yes, please," Archie says, quickly reaching for his wife's hand.

Michael jumps out with the umbrella, and maneuvers them both into the rental car's back seat.

"I think our tank might have run dry," said Archie, his eyes down.

"At least something's dry around here," mutters Gertrude, pushing back her dripping hair. But she's looking at Archie with soft eyes, and feeling the rise of something long lost.

Michael gets out his cell phone and calls their hotel's front desk about the need for a tow truck and petrol. Nobody else in the car speaks.

While they wait for help to arrive Michael tries to foster a bit of conversation. "Horrible weather," he says, sticking to a topic that's safe. "Thankfully, the rain has almost stopped."

There are murmured agreements, but the Ghost of Breakfast Past seems to be reminding each one of them of this morning's encounter, the unkind words and snappy comebacks that had encouraged more of the same.

When the man from the local filling station arrives with a full can of petrol, there are audible sighs of relief.

Back in the hotel's car park, Maggie and Michael watch from their rental car as Gertrude and Archibald step out of their Jag. "Thank you," the older couple mouth in unison, offering regal waves. Hand-in-hand they totter across the puddled cobblestones, their wet clothes clinging to them. Maggie and Michael wait until they have disappeared safely through the hotel's back door, before budging themselves.

Gertrude is in a royal snit, although truth be told she cannot say why. Naturally, being found helpless and bedraggled on a Dorset country road has raised her embarrassment to a level best described as excruciating. Still, she knows that's not what's putting her insides through a grinder. She buttons up her cardigan and sighs with impatience. What on earth has gotten into her?

She and Archie are showered and dressed and sit in their hotel room killing time. She hopes their nine o'clock dinner reservation in the hotel's dining room is late enough to keep them from bumping into Michael and Maggie. There's something about those two that makes her feel small.

"Do you remember the day we met in Chicago, Gertie?" Archie says gently.

Her heart squeezes.

"I thought you were too young for me, remember? You were only eighteen. I was thirty. But you weren't too young for me. Were you, Gertie?"

"Of course not."

"We married when you were nineteen."

"I got out into the world with you, Archie. You

brought me home to England."

He lifted her hand—heavily veined now—and raised it to his lips. "You've ended up with an old man, Gertie," he said. "An old man who forgets things like keeping petrol in the car."

Her face warms. She wonders how many times she has made him feel old and unwanted, this good man who has understood her so completely, who has never faltered in his support of her.

"What do you think happened to us?" Archie continues in that way he has, his eyes staring upward, as if speaking to someone on the ceiling.

Gertrude catches her breath. Is Archie trying to tell her something? Has he had enough of her? "We both got old," she says. "Not just you, Archie."

"Do you still love me, Gertie?"

A rush of tears feels hot on her cheeks. He hands her his handkerchief, white and soft, and waits for her answer.

Gertrude thinks of how he was this morning at the breakfast table, chuckling at Maggie and Michael whenever she mocked them. She sees him this afternoon speaking for them both when Michael asked if they needed a lift. Of course they needed a damned lift. But she, Gertrude, would never have said so. Her husband knew that. He knew that she never needed anyone.

Grief threatens to overwhelm her. She starts to look beyond the wrinkled skin and crinkled eyes to the sweet young man she married. "Of course, I love you, Archie. I'm sorry you've had to ask."

"Remember when James died? Our very last friend?"

Gertrude chokes up.

"I thought then that perhaps it would be good for us; they were all so much older than we are. I thought perhaps we could get back to the way we were when we were younger and not set in our ways. You know?"

She did know. They had been more carefree back then. Not so hoity-toity. Keeping that up had become such an effort.

When her parents were alive, Archie loved visiting their farm. He would get out into the fields with her father and drive the tractor with glee, marveling at Illinois' dry summer weather and hot sunshine. He had liked her parents. But when they hinted that their daughter had married above her station, he told them it was the other way around.

She wonders at her airs and graces, and at the standoffishness that has even kept her husband uncertain, and held him at a distance.

He is seventy-five years old; she is sixty-three. So much life is behind them, so little in front.

Tears flow as Archie pulls her to him.

"Why is it that when somebody thinks they need to put you in your place, they always think that your place is someplace well beneath their place?"

Michael and Maggie are sitting in front of the dining room's cozy fireplace, their noses deep in their menus.

"You have a point," said Michael, looking over the top of his and giving her a wink.

Maggie feels a rush of love for her sweet American husband, a man who always stands ready to support her, who lets her rattle on about her sorrows and woes without complaint. She catches him studying her.

"What is it, Michael?"

"I'm American and you're English. Gertrude is American and Archie is English. We have a few years between us. They have a few years between them. It's surprising how much we have in common."

"They're snooty. We're not snooty. They live in London. We live in Chicago."

He sighs. "Maggie, think of them this afternoon, sopping wet, feeling lost, trying to appear dignified. It could have been us standing there, just as easily."

"What are you trying to say, Michael?"

"What is underneath all of that dignification do you suppose?"

She laughs, and then startles as the fire crackles

loudly and spits out sparks. "She seems fearful and defensive," Maggie realizes, remembering Gertrude's frightened eyes, and the way she appeared to lose power when her hair was soaked. "It's not something you see very often with authentic old-money people."

"Yes, but fearful of what?"

"I don't know." A sudden sympathy for Gertrude strikes Maggie. "What if she feels intimidated by Archie's background, which seems to be quite posh and formal? She might even be overcompensating—"

A hesitant voice speaks from somewhere above their heads, "Good evening."

They look up, shocked.

Archie stands next to their table, holding out his right hand for a handshake. "It's so nice to see you both again."

Gertrude stands slightly behind him, wishing they had ordered room service instead of coming down-stairs. She folds her arms across her chest and shivers. What must they think of her?

"How about joining us for dinner," Michael blurts, ignoring Maggie's kick. "This spot is the warmest place around."

"Thank you. We'd love to." Archie grasps his wife's elbow and quickly pulls out a chair for her.

Gertrude sits down, feeling ridiculous. So much has

happened, and she hasn't had time to catch up with herself. "After getting soaked this afternoon, I still seem to feel the chill."

"Not for much longer," Maggie replies, recognizing Gertrude's discomfort. "It's nice and cozy at this table."

The women exchange cautious smiles.

"I'm sure we'll all find lots to talk about." Archie beams. "We have so much in common."

Maggie finds herself warming to the idea of good conversation with this odd couple, especially since there is so much she wants to find out about them.

Their waiter appears with two more settings of heavy silver cutlery. He hands menus to Archie and Gertrude, and takes their drinks order.

"How about choosing a few hors d'oeuvres to go with them?" Gertrude feels a surge of joy. It's been so many years since she and Archie have done anything impromptu. She glances across at the younger couple, and wonders where they live. It would be nice to have friends in the States.

"Isn't this extraordinary?" Archie murmurs to nobody in particular, his eyes examining the chandelier. "So much like us. Who could have imagined? On a Dorset country road ... in the rain ... on Easter Sunday."

CHECKMATE

Keys rattle and the back door is stabbed a few times before he finds the keyhole. Another delay with more thumps and bumps while he figures out how to work the lock and get into the house. Finally, the door opens and Pete emerges, already wearing the familiar look that says: I know I've been a bad boy, but you'll forgive me.

In the shadows, Lori sits still as stone, wishing him dead.

Tonight, he is so far gone that halfway across their moonlit family room his feet freeze. With eyes at half-mast and jaw slackened he stands helpless, befuddled. Attempts to look down cause him to sway in all directions. He grunts and pats his thighs as if to wake them. Unwilling palms and limp fingers hit and miss their targets as they slap about willy-nilly. A crooked smile appears when he spots her. He struggles to lift his hands high, slurring, "Jeezzuz, Lori. Whatha hell's going on here?"

Lori snaps, "I don't suppose the martinis you've siphoned into yourself caused your shoes to stick to the floor? Must be a virus or something."

Pete delivers a long, blank stare, and then turns on the charm with a come-hither look and leering smile. "C'mon, Babe, be nice."

A moonbeam pushes its way through their blind-covered windows and lands on him as a pool of light, surrounding his head with an eerie halo. His ludicrous face floats before her in a sea of darkness.

Anger threatens to burst out of her like a flame, yet for the first time Lori's despair isn't as sharp and debilitating as it ought to be. Tonight she feels that her own feet are starting to wake up, even as his grow ever more leaden. "I'm going to bed ... alone," she says. Then she lifts herself off the couch.

Pete replaces his grin with a tight-lipped grimace and nods his head slowly, like a wise old sage in the midst of an unfortunate enlightenment. He waves a finger in her direction. "Look at the face on that," he says.

"You might want to look at yourself for a change," says Lori, in a tight, hard voice. "Once more you've driven home along Lake Shore Drive in bumper-to-bumper traffic when you can hardly walk or talk."

"Jeez. There you go again."

"It's a miracle you haven't killed someone."

She has explained this to him dozens of times, as if the concept of not driving when drunk were on a par with quantum physics and, therefore, hard to grasp. She tells herself to stop.

He manages a shaky, menacing step toward her.

Lori's eyes rest on a heavy crystal bowl on the coffee table. For a moment, she pictures hitting him with it full force across the top of his head. It would take a fraction of a second to smash his skull, to take him out, to be rid of him.

Pete shuffles closer. "You think you're so great? You're nothing but a pain in the ass. You always have to find something to bitch about."

The output of so many words proves too much for him. He places his hands on his thighs as though to rest, and stumbles one more step toward her. He peers around the darkened room, rocking on his feet, and squints toward impenetrable corners, seeking out the culprit of this latest outrage.

This is when he is dangerous.

Her skin prickles as she skirts around him and heads toward the stairs, leaving him to seek out his demons alone, in the dark.

Curled up in bed, she does not cry. If she did he might move to comfort her, and she cannot bear the thought of it. She never cries anymore.

Sunlight streaks across the bed as Lori awakens. Most days she operates in a constant state of dread, her heart squeezed into an aching knot, her stomach filled with squirms, her skin stretched around taut nerves, each hair raised, her psyche waiting, waiting, waiting for the next drunken episode, the next betrayal, the next tearful, worthless apology. This morning is no different.

Where is he? she wonders, and then smells the coffee. She grudgingly marvels at how often she manages to feel hung over after a no-drinks night like last night, while Pete, who almost drank himself to death, acts perfectly fine.

She hears the clunk of a cupboard door closing and the clatter of dishes. He is busying himself in the kitchen, making himself useful, being the good guy, the considerate husband. He is showing himself that he is the kind of man he would like to be.

He will expect her to make an appearance.

Pete stands at the sink, his back to her, unaware that he's being watched. He rinses away coffee grinds, wearing his blue pajamas, his dark hair tousled like a child's. He looks so vulnerable she has to look away.

"Hi," she says, in a voice she does not recognize.

He mumbles, "I've made the coffee," and hands her a mug.

She sits at the kitchen table looking out of the window. Silver spangles of frost adorn the lawn and trees. Sunbeams dance across them into the room, dazzling her eyes, warming her feet, making her throat ache.

Pete hesitates before sitting next to her to admire the view. Side-by-side they gaze out into the back yard, sipping their coffees, biding their time.

Lori wiggles her toes and considers feet and legs grown stronger, knowing that they have spent years waiting for her to live, wondering where they will carry her when she seeks to reclaim herself.

Pete chooses this moment to turn his hangdog face toward her like a blight. His trembling fingers reach for hers. His eyes lift, and then lower.

Deep inside of her a living thing twists a painful warning.

"I'm so ashamed, Lori."

Her heartbeat revs up and her legs stiffen. Words tumble out of her, unchecked. "You're not as ashamed as I am for still being here."

For a few moments, he doesn't move.

Then he leans closer. "I'll get a handle on this, Lori." His voice catches on a swell of tears. "I'll do what it takes to make you happy."

She knows this is part of his game, yet his words act as a drug, a painkiller, and she cannot help feeling soothed. She keeps her toes on the floor, but lifts her heels. Her body lightens and relaxes. Her brain floods with uncomfortable joy. She thinks: *Maybe this time he really means it*, and then shoves down the sharp prick of an idea to the contrary.

Pete starts to kiss her fingers, his head tipped forward so that she can barely see his face. Leaning back in her chair, her eyes travel down the gentle curve of his cheek. But when she tilts her head she catches his secret smirk, his upturned lips pressed tight against her hand.

Her back straightens and her feet flatten against the floor. "What's so funny?"

She hears his sigh. His shoulders slump, and his eyes flash the promise of hate. "Don't start again, Lori. I said I'll fix this. What more do you want from me?"

She yanks her hand away. "I can't live like this any-more."

He puts on his poor-me face—the one she sees whenever he tries turning the tables on her—and struggles to his feet like he is older than Methuselah. With his scrambled hair and crumpled pajamas, he looks ridiculous. "There's just no pleasing you," he says.

"It must be nice to have a wife," she retorts, anger spouting in spite of her fear. "Someone who goes out to work herself, but still washes your clothes, cleans the place, buys groceries, makes your meals, keeps track of your social agenda, and puts up with everything else."

"Here we go."

"Someone who is expected to wait around for you forever, like a butler or chauffeur. An indentured servant."

"Give it a rest, Lori."

"You need to leave now, Pete." It flies out of her mouth before she can check it. She is acting like her own worst enemy.

She can feel Pete's stare—cold and bitter—and knows he is preparing for battle.

"I'll get out of here all right," he replies, softly.

She is surprised that Pete is walking away without a fight. She listens to his footfalls on the stairs, waiting for him to see the two suitcases she packed for him during her long vigil last night. That will show him she means what she says this time.

She knows with sudden dread that she should not have done that. She should have just packed her own clothes and quietly vanished. That would have been safer.

Her palms feel clammy, her mouth dry. Her legs feel weak and shaky.

She will tell him he can have this house. He can keep it. If it's the last thing she ever does, she will get her feet moving and run out of here today.

When he comes up from behind, she senses his presence and starts to turn. Her eyes catch a glimpse of the heavy crystal bowl from the coffee table before it hits her full force across the top of her head. It only takes a fraction of a second for him to smash her skull, to take her out, to be rid of her.

BIRDCAGE

Halfway through the roast duck, the fire bell shrieks. I panic. "Shouldn't we be racing out of here?" I scan the dining room. Women in silk frocks and men in summer linens don't appear to have heard anything out of the ordinary. They sit straight-backed, their knives and forks busy.

Bill's right hand cuts through a swath of air. "Headlines in the British papers: 'Honeymooning Yanks trample over Swan Hotel diners during fire drill.'"

A waiter stops to refill our wine glasses. I call out over the din, "What's happening?"

"We have an *awfully* small fire in the kitchen, Madam. I shouldn't worry."

Anglophile Bill mops his mouth to hide his grin. I bet he's already formulating a British understatement story for our friends and family in Boston. They'll love it. "Good thing we didn't act like chickens," he chirps.

The alarm goes silent. Craning my neck toward the windows, I see the fire brigade has arrived. Hoses are being unrolled along the hallway past the dining room's open French doors. The alarm screams and is shut down, fast. Feathers unruffled, the locals dine on.

I mutter, "Headlines in the British papers: 'Tardy Yanks sizzle like Kentucky Fried Chicken during Swan Hotel blaze.'"

"If flying the coop during one's evening meal is considered rude, our goose is already cooked," says Bill, eyeballing the automatic kitchen doors as they open and close willy-nilly.

My stomach tightens. "We're chicken if we run and we're chicken if we stay."

He nods, serious for once. "But, when in Rome … you know?"

We grimly clink glasses, gulp down our chilled Chardonnay, and peck at our roast duck. Even as we glimpse the dousing of kitchen flames, we don't budge from our perches.

WINTER SKIES

Winter's freezing rains and icy streets make Rhonda afraid to take her eyes off her feet lest she step onto a slippery patch and crash to the ground, broken. She clutches her purse to her chest and picks her way along the sidewalk between two-foot high snow banks and rows of lit storefronts, one arm outstretched for balance, the wind whipping her hair out from under her hat to lash at her eyes, making them snap shut.

She steers her feet, never looking up to see where she's heading, afraid that if she lifts her face, she will wander onto that fatal stretch of ice.

She doesn't admit this.

Turning the corner, her eyes down, she slips hard into the gutter. Helpless on her back, she faces the sky.

A burly man wearing a red and white striped apron rushes toward her. He bends over and holds out his hand. "Are you all right?" he asks.

Rhonda feels sick, but says, "I'm all right. I just need a minute to collect myself." She notices the goosebumps that decorate his bare arms and realizes it's Dan from the butcher shop. "I was on my way to see you," she says.

He helps her to her feet. "Sounds like something important, you coming here today, and in this weather." When he smiles, his teeth wink clean and bright.

She wants to tell him that she is more afraid of sitting alone with her thoughts than of walking into the village in this horrible weather. Instead, she says, "I need stew meat."

Dan's butcher shop is deserted, just like the streets, but so warm she starts to feel woozy. He pulls out a black stool from behind the counter and pats it three times. "Sit here and catch your breath."

Rhonda catches a whiff of bleach, sharp and tangy. She admires the store's scrubbed walls and polished glass cabinets filled with pale cuts of poultry and rosy meats, all laid out on stainless steel trays. She stares down at the white tile floor, and the trail of dark footprints she brought in with her.

"Don't worry about that," Dan says. "There's nothing to be done for it on a day like today."

He hands her a glass of water.

She drinks it down like a shot.

"What's wrong?" he says gently. "Tell me."

Words stay trapped in her throat. She shrugs.

She can't keep her eyes off his hands, which are broad and strong. She thinks that his hands know how to make mincemeat out of a side of beef. She pictures her husband.

The butcher checks his watch, and walks to the front of the store. He rolls down the window blinds. He puts up the closed sign and locks the door. "No point in staying open when there's nobody else out looking for fresh meat today."

He stands in front of her. "Tell me, Rhonda. What is it?"

Tears pop into her eyes. She blinks them back.

He slowly leans forward and plants a soft kiss on her mouth.

A surge of heat threatens to overtake her. She unbuttons her coat and opens it wide. "Who would have thought?" she murmurs, raising her eyes to meet his.

Under overcast skies, behind Rhonda's gray stone house, Dan counts out the minutes. He wonders what it would be like to live in a grand place like this, in such a secluded setting, with not a single prying eye leveled upon it.

He himself prefers living above the butcher shop in his bright, cozy apartment, surrounded by his dearest things. The air up there holds the faintest tinge of raw meat, and that too is a comfort.

Overall, he's pretty satisfied with his lot. For three years he's lived dead center in the village, in full view of his customers, many of whom drive in from miles around. They like to say he's the best butcher they've ever had. His quiet demeanor and polite smile make him a man to be trusted. It's interesting how they don't really see him.

The wind nips at his cheeks. He pulls his scarf higher, and glances at his watch. He should have worn a warmer coat. He yearns for the hot days of summer, the hotter the better, so far as he's concerned. Those are the days that really make him come alive.

He moves across the patio, clicks open the French doors, and steps inside. Just as he expected, the ground floor is deserted and shadowy in the winter light. Glad of the warmth, he creeps toward the staircase, the sound of splashing water leading the way.

He thinks: This a piece of cake.

From the doorway of the master bathroom, he peers through the shower's beveled glass door. Through the steam, he can make out a distorted figure, tall and dark, singing some sort of dirge, mostly off key. Dan takes a silent step forward.

Abruptly, the water shuts off.

A hand reaches out of the stall and starts groping for a towel.

The back room of Dan's butcher shop is as pristine as the front. He makes sure of it. Even though they never walk back here, his customers will imagine its cleanness. He wouldn't want to disappoint.

An Arctic blast sweeps in through the cracked-open window behind him. Dan shivers. He sniffs the air for lingering traces of bleach before turning to close it with a bang.

He hears the tick of the wall clock.

Many of his customers will want meat and potatoes for dinner tonight, their favorite comfort foods. He had better speed up in case there's a rush.

The Rolling Stones' "Sympathy for the Devil" floats out of the radio. He revs up the volume and hums along, tapping his foot against the white tile floor, his smile sickle-shaped like a curved crescent moon.

This morning he is preparing his sage flavored sausage, a winner with his customers. The meat grinder churns out the last of the minced meat. Dan picks up the sausage casings, and looks around to see what comes next.

He opens up in half an hour.

Mounds of stew meat are laid out on stainless steel trays ready for the display cases. A batch of sweeter meat needs his attention, but will soon land in his freezer.

Dan wonders about Rhonda's life. He sees her upturned face, her soft, full lips, and feels himself stir.

He just can't get enough of her.

WE HAVE A PRODUCT FOR THAT

We know that you look
too fat, too thin
too tall, too short
too bony, too stocky
too not right
We have a product for that

We know that your hair is
Too curly, too straight
Too thick, too thin
Too dry, too oily
Too not right
We have a product for that

We know that your skin is
Too pale, too dark
Too oily, too dry
Too freckled, too lined,
Too not right
We have a product for that

We know that
Your lips are too thin, too thick
Your brows are too thick, too thin
Your nose is too wide, too narrow
Your teeth are too crooked, too stained
We have a product for that

We know that
Your breasts are too small, too low
Your thighs are too big, too blubbery
Your stomach is too round, too loose
Your body is too hairy, too mottled
We have a product for that

We know that you feel
Too happy, too sad
Too imperfect, too ugly
Too insecure, too despairing
Too not right
We have a product for that

We know that our products can be
Too dangerous
Too likely to not work
Too likely to contribute to your suicide
Too not right
We'll soon have a product for that

ABOUT THE AUTHOR

Christine Todd was born and raised in County Durham, England, but lived most of her life in the American Midwest, most recently Chicago. Her short fiction and articles have appeared in various US and UK publications. She is author of the novel, *Pins*. *Tornado Days* is her first collection of short stories.

Visit her website

christine-todd.com

Pins
A Novel
"*Pins* is a beautifully written jewel
of a novel...a great, uplifting read."
— Jerry Cleaver, author, *Immediate Fiction*
christine todd

PRAISE FOR THE NOVEL *PINS*

"Pins is a beautifully written jewel of a novel ... a great, uplifting read."

—Jerry Cleaver, *Immediate Fiction*

"A sprightly first novel ... a witty writer ... good at delineating characters and their motivations."

—*Shepherd Express,* Milwaukee

"I love the story and the humor. [The author] is brilliant at introducing both comedic and tender moments."

—Sally Zigmond, *Hope against Hope*

"This is a witty, modern story set in Chicago ... the writing is first class ... it comes highly recommended."

—Rebecca Tope, Cotswold murder mystery series

"Plenty of humor ... snappy style ... a good read and definitely recommended."

—Kathleen McGurl, *Brief Bits About Books,* UK

"Pins is a cracking read ... funny and kind and warm. The story is great, the characters are well rounded and believable. Ms. Todd's writing is clear and simple and easy to read. I loved it! A delightful, absorbing book ... highly recommended."

—Jane Smith, *How Publishing Really Works,* UK

"Detailed and engaging from the off ... Christine Todd is the new Deborah Moggach."

—Philip Turner, *Screentrade Magazine,* UK